D1128582

A Little Note for Mom

Because this is the first time I'm going to go so long without seeing her, poor dear... Anyway, I'll be fine, I'll have **My friends**

YEAAH!

I can't wait, I can already see us at the beach...

Me · Mary Emily · Mina · Karen

And she'll be with Richard. So I'll leave a little note for him too.

And... OMG...

THE CAT!

I forgot the cat! We'll need another commando operation to get him into his carrier!

OK, stay calm... Just draw up a

THE MAN WITH THE VEST MADE OF **DEAD SHEEP**

Dear Mommy,
I haven't even left yet, ginormously... (ha ha) But anyway, note to tell you that I'll be thinking of you, that I'll take good care of the cat, and that I think you'll also have a great vacation. After all, this is your first vacation with Richard! WHOOT! IN LUUUV!
And anyway, we'll see each other the 24th at the Pine Ridge Convention.
(me) Your favorite daughter (Lou)

P.S.: Don't forget to water the plants: the big one by the door once per week and the little ones on my balcony~~just~~ ~~~~ You'll do fine.

for Richard

Richard,
I'm going on a seaside holiday. I'm leaving you alone with my mom. She's the only one I have, so be careful with her. (joking)
If you get bored of her, just annoy her, usually that riles her up, and she'll start sulking and then you'll get a little peace. So, that's my advice. I'm telling you this because you're a good guy.

Hugs. Your "stepdaughter."

P.S.: Kidding aside, watch out for Mom, at crosswalks and stuff... She is REALLY upset.

(Don't forget to give them their notes!!!)

CAPTURE PLAN

NOTE: BE CAREFUL: SOME SCRATCHES ARE INEVITABLE!

OK: some definitions

OUR TARGET

TOP SECRET!
THE ANIMAL (SEE INTELLIGENCE REPORT 545-P IN THE ATTACHED DOCUMENT.)
WARNING: HE IS AS CUTE AS HE IS DANGEROUS!

BATHROOM (MAP)

pile of underwear right next to an EMPTY CLOTHES BASKET
(standard model) IN GENUINE PINK PLASTIC

SO

we move on now to: THE SECOND PART OF THE PLAN

INTELLIGENCE REPORT 545-P

PSEUDONYMS: Crusty Joe, Minou, Mount Bob, Giga, Henry Gale, Son of Tao, Caramel Pepperoni, Little Booboo... etc... etc...
WEAPONS: Claws, fangs
SPECIAL SKILLS: Disappears when you're looking for him

OK on further thought, I dunno if it's such a great plan... Anyway, we shall see...

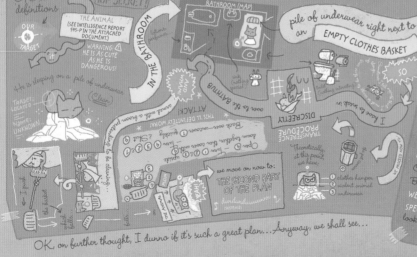

Lou! ④ ♡

The Perfect Summer

JULIEN NEEL

Glenview Public Library
1930 Glenview Road
Glenview, Illinois 60025

GRAPHIC UNIVERSE™ · MINNEAPOLIS · NEW YORK

TO MY BROTHER

Story and art by Julien Neel

Translation by Carol Klio Burrell

First American edition published in 2012 by Graphic Universe™.

Lou! by Julien Neel © 2007 — Glénat Editions
© 2012 Lerner Publishing Group, Inc., for the U.S. edition

Graphic Universe™ is a trademark of Lerner Publishing Group, Inc.

All U.S. rights reserved. International copyright secured. No part of this book may be reproduced, stored in a retrieval system, or transmitted in any form or by any means——electronic, mechanical, photocopying, recording, or otherwise—— without the prior written permission of Lerner Publishing Group, Inc., except for the inclusion of brief quotations in an acknowledged review.

Graphic Universe™
A division of Lerner Publishing Group, Inc.
241 First Avenue North
Minneapolis, MN 55401 U.S.A.

Website address: www.lernerbooks.com

Library of Congress Cataloging-in-Publication Data

Neel, Julien.
   [Idylles. English]
   The perfect summer / [story and art by] Julien Neel ; [translation by Carol Klio Burrell]. — 1st American ed.
      p.   cm. — (Lou! ; #4)
   Summary: Lou and her friends find romance when they spend summer vacation at a posh beach house, while Lou's mother travels on a book tour for her new science fiction novel.
   ISBN 978–0–7613–8780–0 (lib. bdg. : alk. paper)
   1. Graphic novels. [1. Graphic novels. 2. Summer—Fiction. 3. Vacations—Fiction. 4. Dating (Social customs)—Fiction. 5. Mothers and daughters—Fiction.] I. Burrell, Carol Klio. II. Title.
   PZ7.7.N44Pe 2012
   741.5'944—dc23   2012002988

Manufactured in the United States of America
1 – DP – 7/15/12

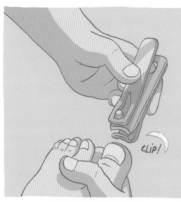

CLIP!

THIS IS THE FIRST SUMMER I'VE SPENT WITHOUT HER.

YEAH, BUT IT'S ALSO THE FIRST SUMMER YOU'VE SPENT WITH ME...

HEH HEH.

AND YOU KNOW WHAT? MAYBE WE'LL GET TO HAVE A REAL ROMANTIC GETAWAY!

HUH?

I RAN THIS PAST MY EDITOR: AN AUTHOR TOUR, BOOK SIGNINGS ACROSS THE COUNTRY...

AND HE'LL PAY ALL THE EXPENSES.

FANCY RESTAURANTS, SWANK HOTELS...

LIKE IN JAMES BOND!

AND BEST OF ALL:

I CAN BRING MY GUY.

THAT'S ME, RIGHT?

OF COURSE, SILLY.

COOL!

LIKE IN JAMES BOND, YOU SAY?

TOTALLY.

BUT PROBABLY WITHOUT THE LICENSE TO KILL.

I'LL ASK. YOU NEVER KNOW...

SMACK!

DO YOU THINK SHE'S THINKING ABOUT ME TOO, AT LEAST A LITTLE?

EARTH TO LOU! YOU THERE?

HUH? WHAT? UH, SORRY, I...

MAN, IT'S WEIRD. I KEEP THINKING ABOUT MY MOM...

YEAH, THAT'S WEIRD.

YOUR FIRST VACATION WITHOUT HER! ENJOY!

YEAH, I SHOULD, BUT...

RELAX...

YOU KNOW HOW LUCKY YOU ARE?

TOTALLY.

GIIIIRLS! LOOK AT ALL THE LOVELY STONE TERRACES!

HEEEENRY? DID YOU SEE THE LOVELY STONE TERRACES?

GRNT.

SO PRETTY, RIGHT?

AND YOU'RE SURE THIS IS THE RIGHT ROAD?!

WELL, IF YOU SAY WE'RE ON THE RIGHT ROAD, WE'RE ON THE RIGHT ROAD.

I'LL TRUST YOU, HENRY...

LIKE OUR THERAPIST ADVISED.

HEY, WEREN'T YOU BEGGING TO GO ON THIS TRIP?

IT'S OK. IT'LL PASS.

ARE YOU MOPING ALREADY?

I'D GIVE ANYTHING FOR A VACATION WITHOUT MY MOTHER...

MARY EMILY! PUT ON YOUR SEAT BELT!

THE SEAT BELT IS INFRINGING ON MY PERSONAL FREEDOMS!

♪ AND WE'RE OFF! ♪ WATCH YOUR TONE, YOUNG LADY!

WHAT, DO YOU ENJOY HUMILIATING ME IN FRONT OF MY FRIENDS?

HENRY, SAY SOMETHING!

WE'RE HERE.

OH.

GOOD JOB, HENRY. YOU...

YOU WERE RIGHT, HENRY. WE WERE ON THE RIGHT ROAD.

I TRUSTED YOU, YOU KNOW...

AND THAT'S THE MAIN THING: TRUST.

4

WHOA.

HEY, CHECK OUT ALL THE TREES AND STUFF.

THAT COTTAGE IS DREAMY!

ISN'T IT?

PFFT...

ARCHIBALD PARMENTIER DESIGNED IT. HE WAS A FAMOUS ARCHITECT FROM THE 1960s...

LAY OFF. SOUNDS LIKE YOU'RE BRAGGING...

OH, NO, NOT AT ALL!

HEY! IT'S JUST LIKE SNOOP DOGG'S POOL!

DID YOU HEAR HOW YOUR DAUGHTER SPOKE TO ME?

THIS LITTLE BRIDGE ROCKS.

GRNT?

ADMIT IT: YOU'VE NEVER LOVED ME!

NEVER!

GRNT.

HOW COULD YOU SAY THAT?

CHECK THIS OUT, A STRAIGHT-UP CLASSY COLUMN.

ALL YOU CARE ABOUT IS YOUR CRAPPY MONEY!

SPLOOF!

HENRY! SAY SOMETHING!!

HEY!

SPLOOF!

HENRY?

ARE YOU...CRYING OVER THERE?

WHA?!

OOPSIE!

I'M SORRY, HENRY, I...

HEH.

SPLOOF!

ALL RIGHT! IT'S VACATION TIME!

IF I CATCH HER, THE GOTH IS A DEAD WOMAN!

YEAH!

I DIDN'T MEAN TO DOUBT YOUR MANLINESS...

FIRST ONE TO THE ROOM GETS TO PICK HER BED!

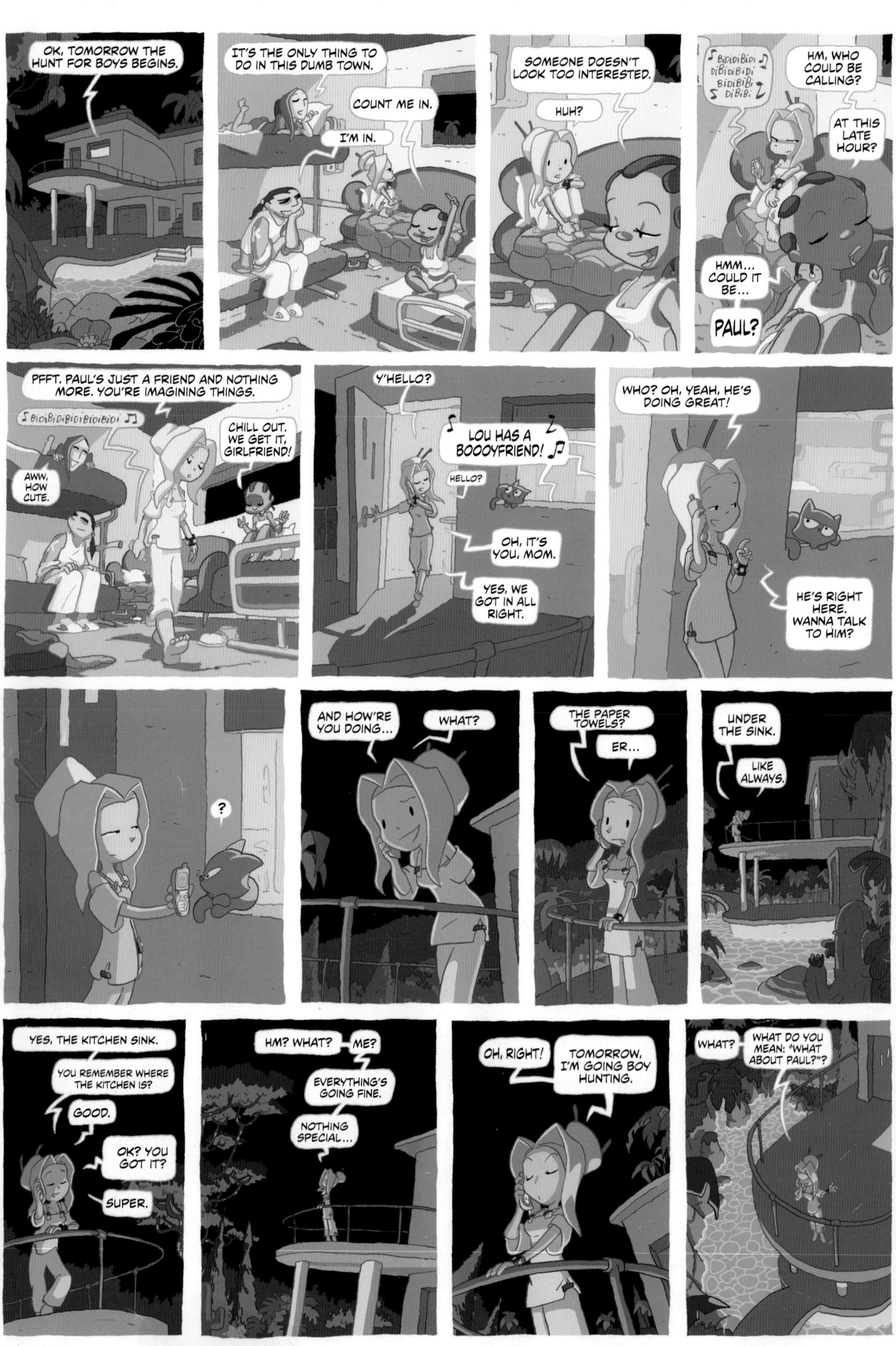
OK, TOMORROW THE HUNT FOR BOYS BEGINS.
IT'S THE ONLY THING TO DO IN THIS DUMB TOWN.
COUNT ME IN.
I'M IN.
SOMEONE DOESN'T LOOK TOO INTERESTED.
HUH?
BIDIBIDI DIBIDIBIDI BIDIBIBI DIBIBI
HM, WHO COULD BE CALLING?
AT THIS LATE HOUR?
HMM... COULD IT BE...
PAUL?
PFFT. PAUL'S JUST A FRIEND AND NOTHING MORE. YOU'RE IMAGINING THINGS.
BIDIBIDIBIDIBIDIBIDI
CHILL OUT. WE GET IT, GIRLFRIEND!
AWW, HOW CUTE.
Y'HELLO?
LOU HAS A BOOOYFRIEND!
HELLO?
OH, IT'S YOU, MOM.
YES, WE GOT IN ALL RIGHT.
WHO? OH, YEAH, HE'S DOING GREAT!
HE'S RIGHT HERE. WANNA TALK TO HIM?
?
AND HOW'RE YOU DOING...
WHAT?
THE PAPER TOWELS?
ER...
UNDER THE SINK.
LIKE ALWAYS.
YES, THE KITCHEN SINK.
YOU REMEMBER WHERE THE KITCHEN IS?
GOOD.
OK? YOU GOT IT?
SUPER.
HM? WHAT?
ME?
EVERYTHING'S GOING FINE.
NOTHING SPECIAL...
OH, RIGHT!
TOMORROW, I'M GOING BOY HUNTING.
WHAT?
WHAT DO YOU MEAN: "WHAT ABOUT PAUL?"?

YEAH, YOU KNOW: PAUL...

HER FRIEND WHO'S ON A WEIRD HAWAII KICK WITH HIS UKULELE, SARONG, AND ALL.

OOOHH, RIIIGHT. THE GUY SHE WROTE THAT LETTER TO...

THAT'S THE ONE. ANYWAY, GO FIGURE, SHE TELLS ME SHE DOESN'T LIKE HIM OR ANYTHING...

THAT HE IS JUST A FRIEND...

MM... YEAH...

YEAH, WHATEVER...

SURE.

ANYWAY, IT'S NONE OF OUR BUSINESS...

THEY SAID THEY'D SEND A CAR TO TAKE US TO THE BOOK FESTIVAL.

A LIMOUSINE, I BET...

LIKE IN JAMES BOND, I TELL YOU!

HEY, YOU THE WRITER?

UH...IS THE BOOK FESTIVAL FAR?

FESTIVAL? YOU KNOW, IT'S JUST A LITTLE TWO-WEEK PROMOTIONAL EVENT...

OUR THING IS MOSTLY DISCOUNT SMALL APPLIANCES.

BUT WE GOTTA GET THE FOLKS OUT HERE SOMEHOW...

SO WE BRING IN SOME ARTSY TYPES LIKE YOU...

LAST YEAR WE HAD THAT GUY WHO PLAYED THE GRAPES IN THE AD FOR THAT FRUIT JUICE, YOU KNOW?

FUNNY GUY, YOU SHOULDA SEEN IT!

SO PEOPLE COME TO THE STORE TO SEE THE CELEB, AND WE UNLOAD A WASHER-DRYER ON 'EM...

C'MON, YOUR BOOKS ARE OVER BY THE MICROWAVES.

THERE YOU GO.

IF YOU NEED ANYTHING, A GLASS OF WATER OR SOMETHING...

WELL, I'LL LEAVE YOU TO IT. YOUR FANS AWAIT.

Author of SIDERA signing from 3 to 6 PM

Out-of-this-world prices!

Cosmic Sales

Author of SIDERA signing from 3 to 6 PM

I SWEAR, THAT EDITOR OF MINE, I'M GONNA--

SHH, HERE COMES A FAN.

'SCUSE ME?

IS THE GUY WHO PLAYED THE GRAPES GONNA BE HERE?

7

HEY HEY!

FRUIT JUICE, ANYONE?

MISTER JUICE!

AS SEEN ON TV!

I REALLY FEEL SORRY FOR YOU, MISTER JUICE.

OK, KAREN, LET HIM BE. THE GUY'S JUST MAKING A LIVING...

WE'RE JUST TALKING.

SERIOUSLY, I'M TIRED OF BEING A SILLY ROMANTIC...

HUH?

THE LOU WHO WAITED BY THE PHONE FOR A THOUSAND YEARS, HOPING FOR SOMETHING TO HAPPEN IN HER LOVE LIFE? THAT LOU IS OVER!

WHAT'S SHE GOING ON ABOUT?

DUNNO...

NOW I'M OUT THERE. I'M ALIVE. I EXIST!

IT'S SUMMER AFTER ALL!

AND I'LL SAY IT AGAIN: PAUL IS JUST A FRIEND!

NOTHING MORE.

HEY, GIRLS! LOOK AT THIS!

I GOT A BUNCH OF JUICE BOXES OFF THAT DOPE OVER THERE.

LA VIE EST BELLE! LA VITA È BELLA! LIFE IS BEAUTIFUL!

KAREN AND I ARE GETTING OUR HAIR DONE. WE'LL MEET YOU AND LITTLE MISS SUNSHINE AT NOON ON THE DOCK.

OK, LATER.

SO, BOY HUNTING TIME?

HUH?

WHAT?

ANY ADVICE, ANY SPECIAL TECHNIQUES?

UM...

SURE...

GENERALLY, I PRETEND TO FAINT AROUND SOME GUY WHO LOOKS GOOD. I ACT LIKE A LITTLE FRAGILE THING IN DISTRESS. THAT USUALLY GETS THINGS STARTED...

OH?

LOOK AT THE PRETTY BUNCH OVER THERE.

AND THEY HAVE VESPAS.

BONUS!

THAT WILL PISS OFF MY PARENTS, PLUS IT'S THE BEST WAY TO GET AROUND TOWN...

WAIT...WEIRD...THAT GUY IN THE MIDDLE...I...I...

THE HOT ONE?

HE'S REALLY CHANGED, BUT...

I'M PRETTY SURE THAT'S...

TRISTAN?!

YOU KNOW HIM?

BUT...IT'S NOT POSSIBLE! WHAT'S TRISTAN DOING HERE?

WOW.

LET'S GO ASK HIM...

ARE YOU NUTS?

IF IT'S NOT HIM, I'LL LOOK STUPID!

AND IF IT IS HIM, I'LL LOOK EVEN MORE STUPID!

OH, I GET IT NOW.

YOU GET WHAT?

YOUR LITTLE SPEECH ABOUT HOW LIFE IS SO BEAUTIFUL AND THIS IS THE NEW LOU WHO'S FINALLY GETTING OFF HER REAR? THAT WAS JUST NOISE.

YEAH, NO, BUT-- THAT COULD BE TRISTAN!

HE WAS MY NEIGHBOR FOR YEARS. I WAS CRAZY ABOUT HIM, AND WE WERE SORT OF GOING OUT, AND THEN HE MOVED TO ANOTHER CITY.

BUT IT ISN'T THAT BAD, BECAUSE I'M OVER HIM NOW.

OK, GREAT.

HOW'S THAT GREAT?

YOU'RE OVER HIM, RIGHT?

YEAH, I...

ALL RIGHT, THEN.

MARY EM! NO!

DON'T...

THESE SANDALS WERE MADE FOR WALKIN'!

OH! MY HEAD'S ALL DIZZY!

HEY!

ARE YOU ALL RIGHT?

WH-WHERE AM I?

YOU LIKE?

HMM.

CAN YOU BELIEVE THIS? THIS CUT-RATE BARBER GAVE ME CURLS!

I AM A HAIR STYLISTE...

THEY LOOK FABULOUS ON YOU.

SHE'S RIGHT, ACTUALLY.

DOES SHE THINK I'M SHIRLEY TEMPLE OR SOMETHING?

MARY EMILY IS GOING TO MAKE FUN OF ME...

NO WAY...

BWAHA! LOOK AT THAT FRO!

?!?

T-TRISTAN?

HEY, MINA!

HOW...?

WILD, HUH?

YEAH, CAN YOU BELIEVE OUR LUCK?

I FAINTED AND POOF, I FELL INTO YOUR PAL TRISTAN'S ARMS!

I'M OVER AT THE CAMPGROUND, WITH MY BUDS.

YOU FAINTED?

LET IT GO.

WE'RE GOING TO THE BEACH. WANNA COME?

MOVE OVER, I'M DRIVING.

HUH?

C'MON, GET ON.

UH, YEAH, BUT...

EVERYBODY READY?

WHATEVER, LET'S GO.

LAST ONE TO THE BEACH PAYS FOR THE ICE CREAM!

...ANYWAY, WHY NOT?

ICE WATER?

SORRY, I DON'T HAVE ANY.

HERE, HAVE SOME SODAS...

THEY'RE WARM, THOUGH...

'CAUSE THE FRIDGE IS BROKEN.

SORRY.

THE A/C IS BROKEN TOO.

YOU KNOW, I'M REALLY THRILLED TO HAVE YOU HERE. I LOVE YOUR BOOK!

YOU'VE READ IT?

SURE!

SOME PARTS REALLY REMINDED ME OF THE NORBLUK TRILOGY, WHICH OF COURSE YOU KNOW...

UH, NO.

IS THERE ANY WARM SODA FOR ME?

YOU'VE REALLY BEEN INFLUENCED BY THE LATEST SCIENCE FICTION NOVELS, HUH?

THE LATEST NOVELS?

SOME SODA?

YEAH...

THE LOST GALAXY, THE COSMIC DEFENDER, THE ANDROMEDA CYCLE...

SO, YOU SEE...

NOT AT ALL.

ANY MORE SODA?

NOPE.

SO YOU MUST ALSO BE A BIG FAN OF SCROLL OF THE CYBER-POPES.

OF WHAT?

YOU DON'T KNOW SCROLL OF THE CYBER-POPES?

DOESN'T RING A BELL, SORRY.

BUT YOU MUST READ SCROLL OF THE CYBER-POPES.

MUST.

SLURP.

OK, I'M GOING TO GO SORT INVENTORY IN THE BACK. CALL ME IF ANYBODY COMES IN.

UH, OK.

YOU WANNA FINISH MY WARM SODA?

11

HEEENNRYY? WOULD YOU LIKE SOME MELON?

GRNT.

IT'S DEEE-LI-CIOUS!

STILL WORKING, MR. GARSON?

HEY, WOMEN, YOU COMING?

GRNT?

BUT I FEEL NAKED WITHOUT MY TRACKSUIT...

JUST TAKE BABY STEPS...

WANT TO BORROW MY TANK TOP?

I WOULDN'T DARE...

♪ I DARE YOU! ♪

OH, GIRLS, YOU'RE UP?

DO YOU WANT TO EAT? I HAVE SOME DEEE-LI-CIOUS MELON...

UM, MARY EMILY DIDN'T TELL YOU LAST NIGHT?

SEE, UM...

WE'RE GOING ON A PICNIC THIS AFTERNOON...

AH.

SORRY.

AND MELON IS GROSS.

NO WORRIES!

THE IMPORTANT THING IS THAT YOU HAVE FUN!

FINE, WE DON'T NEED YOUR BLESSING!

HEY, MR. HENRY! HOW'S IT GOING?

GRNT?

WATCH OUT FOR THOSE DELINQUENT BOYS DOWN BY THE CAMPGROUNDS...

WITH THEIR HORRIBLE LITTLE ITALIAN MOTORBIKES...

YEAH, WATCH OUT.

AREN'T YOU HUNGRY, HENRY?

THE MELON IS DEE-LI-CIOUS, YOU KNOW.

WHAT'S TAKING THOSE GIRLS SO LONG?

THEY'RE GIRLS. YOU KNOW.

NO, I DON'T, ACTUALLY...

WE AREN'T ALL LOVE EXPERTS LIKE YOU, DON JUAN.

HMPH.

I HAVEN'T GONE OUT WITH ALL THAT MANY GIRLS...

YEAH, BUT YOU GET HERE AND ONE JUST FALLS INTO YOUR ARMS!

PAH!

OH, I FEEL FAINT!

ARE YOU ALL RIGHT, M'LADY?

MY, WHAT BEAUTIFUL EYES!

AND YOU'VE ALREADY GONE OUT WITH HER FRIEND, THE REALLY PRETTY LITTLE BLONDE...

LOU?

YEAH, BUT IT WAS WHEN WE WERE STILL LITTLE KIDS.

SO THAT MAKES TWO GIRLS...

...MORE THAN THE REST OF US PUT TOGETHER.

BUT I...

YOUR COUSIN DOESN'T COUNT.

NEVER MIND...

ANYWAY, LOU ACTS SO DISTANT. IT'S WEIRD...

SO IT'S OVER BETWEEN YOU TWO?

BEATS ME.

BACK THEN I DIDN'T THINK I WAS INTERESTED IN GIRLS.

YOU MEAN YOU MIGHT BE...

NAH!

SHH! THEY'RE HERE!

HEY!

UH...SO, ANYONE SEE THE GAME LAST NIGHT?

13

THIS WAY.

WHERE ARE YOU TAKING US?

IT'S A SURPRISE!

WOW, IT'S STEEP!

THAT'S WHY NO ONE COMES HERE!

...EXCEPT US!

WHOO!

HEY.

HEY.

WE HAVEN'T EVEN SPOKEN TO EACH OTHER YET. WEIRD.

WHAT'VE YOU BEEN UP TO?

UH...

NOTHING SPECIAL...

YOU KNOW...I USED TO THINK ABOUT YOU A LOT...

OUCH!

HEY, I SEE WHAT YOU'RE UP TO.

PRETENDING TO TRIP SO YOU CAN FALL INTO HIS ARMS, NICE TRY, BUT THAT'S MY MOVE!

UH, NO, WAIT...

HUH?

SO YOU'RE OVER HIM, HUH?

I SWEAR, I...

I DON'T THINK SO.

ER...I'M GOING OVER THERE...

CAN YOU BELIEVE IT? THEY'RE FIGHTING OVER HIM.

DISGUSTING!

HERE IT IS!

WOW!

LET THE PICNIC BEGIN!

COUNTRY HAM, COUNTRY MELON...

COOL! MELON!

I BROUGHT THE DRINKS.

THEY'RE WARM BUT GOOD...

HOW'S YOUR MOM? STILL PLAYING VIDEO GAMES ALL THE TIME?

NAH, SHE'S IN LOVE. SHE'S OVER THAT NOW.

YEAH, I'M OVER THEM TOO!

BIP!

I'M NOT TRYING TO SAY THAT TRAVELING WITH YOU ISN'T SUPER FUN...

HOLD ON, DON'T MESS ME UP...

OK, I'LL SAVE AND TURN THE GAME OFF.

BIP.

NOW WHAT?

JUST A SECOND!

I'M SAVING, HOLD ON...

OH DEAR, IS SIR GRUMPY BECAUSE I MADE HIM WAIT FIVE SECONDS?

WELL, WITH THE BIG CROWDS COMING TO YOUR BOOK SIGNINGS, YOU NEED TO UNWIND.

HEY! THAT WAS A HORRIBLE THING TO SAY!

UH...I...

SORRY, I...

IT WAS ABSOLUTELY HORRIBLE OF YOU!

NO, BUT...I DIDN'T MEAN TO...

IF YOU'RE NOT HAPPY, YOU CAN GET RIGHT OFF THIS TRAIN, RIGHT?

RIGHT?

I GET IT!

I FORGOT WHAT A BIG HEAD YOU HAVE, MR. ETERNAL GRAD STUDENT.

BUT...

IT'S BEEN AGES SINCE I'VE EVEN SEEN YOU STUDYING, ANYWAY...

AND THIS ISN'T THE TIME TO WIND ME UP--THE NEXT STOP IS THE MORTSVILLE BOOK FESTIVAL. MORTSVILLE, THE VILLAGE WHERE I GREW UP AND WHERE MY MOTHER LIVES...

PLEASE, I'M...

...I'M SO SORRY...

AND I DON'T KNOW IF YOU REMEMBER MY MOTHER, BUT THIS SORRY EXCUSE FOR A BOOK TOUR IS JUST THE SORT OF THING SHE'LL USE TO EXPLAIN LONG AND LOUD HOW I'M A FAILURE, AND THAT I SHOULD HAVE LISTENED TO HER AND WORKED IN THE POST OFFICE AND MARRIED CLEMENT FIFFER.

UHHH?

I DON'T KNOW WHAT TO DO.

I KNOW.

HOLD ME.

15

OK, ENOUGH, OK.

YOU'LL SEE HIM TOMORROW.

HMPH.

SHH, HENRY!

I THINK I HEAR THE GIRLS!

GRNT?

GIIIIIRLLLS?

IS THAT YOU?

SEE YOU TOMORROW?

HMM?

UH, SURE.

LATER.

HEY, GUYS? WE GOING OR WHAT?

?

ROAR!

HEY, HEY, MINA. YOU GO, GIRL!

MINA WINS FIRST PRIZE IN THE BOY HUNT!

INDEED!

LATER.

COF

VROAAAR!

HEELLOOO?

GIIIIRLLLS?

I'M TELLING YOU, HE SAID SUCH NICE THINGS TO ME!

AHHH, GIRLS! IT IS YOU!

I WAS...STARTING TO WORRY.

OH YEAH? AS IF YOU REALLY CARE.

AND YOU? DIDN'T I SEE YOU TALKING WITH TRISTAN?

YEAH, SORT OF.

TSK

THERE'S LOTS OF MELON LEFT. I THOUGHT WE COULD ALL EAT TOGETHER...

GREAT IDEA.

I'M GOING TO BED. YOU HAVE FUN.

SORRY, I'M GOING TO BED TOO...

WOW, MY LEGS ARE ALL TREMBLY!

?

GOOD NIGHT, MR. HENRY!

GRNT.

SO? UP FOR A FRUIT PARTY?

...SURE. LOU AND I ARE UP FOR IT, RIGHT?

...YEAH.

GRAND!

SHALL WE SET UP A TABLE BY THE POOL?

HEEENRY? WHAT DO YOU THINK?

HEENRY?

GRNT?

16

SO. TELL ME...

I HAVE A QUESTION...

JUST BETWEEN US...

HEY.

?

YEAH, GIANNI?

YOU KNOW...

OK, I'VE NEVER REALLY KISSED A GIRL BEFORE...

SO I WANTED TO ASK...

OK, IT'S WEIRD... MY ARMS ARE ALL FLOPPY AND SWEATY...

SEE?

YOU HAVE EXPERIENCE AND ALL...

STOP RIGHT THERE. I'M NOT AN EXPERT.

BUT STILL, ARE THESE SYMPTOMS NORMAL, YOU THINK?

ARGH, I DUNNO! I GUESS YOU'RE IN LOVE.

IN...IN LOVE?

YEESH. YOU MADE ME MESS UP!

WHAT DO YOU MEAN, "I GUESS"?

OK, I'LL TELL YOU. I'VE KISSED SOME GIRLS, BUT I NEVER FELT LIKE THAT...

NOT EVEN WITH LOU, WHEN YOU WENT OUT WITH HER WAY BACK WHEN?

NOT BACK THEN, NO.

MM-HMM. AND NOW?

ARE YOU GETTING SOME SYMPTOMS FROM HER?

ARRGH...SHUT UP, GIANNI! YOU'RE BEING A PAIN!

AND YOU MADE ME MESS UP AGAIN.

OOOKAY!

YEAH, I GET IT...

I AM IN LOVE!

OH, COOL.

BLAH BLAH BLAH.

♪ Giiirrls! ♪
Brekkies!

ARE YOU TRYING TO MAKE US FAT OR WHAT?

YOU WANT US TO GET BIG AND SLOPPY LIKE YOU? IS THAT YOUR GOAL IN LIFE?

THAT'S ENOUGH.

WHAT'S WITH YOU?

LEMME GO! LEMME GO!

SO, WHERE WAS I?

YOU WERE TELLING ME ABOUT YOUR STRANGE SYMPTOMS AROUND GIANNI.

OH, RIGHT. ARE YOU SURE YOU NEVER FELT ANYTHING LIKE THAT WHEN YOU WERE GOING OUT WITH TRISTAN?

NOT THE POOL! NOT THE POOL!

NOPE...

NOT BACK THEN, NO...

WHAT ABOUT NOW?

WELLL...

SPLATCH!

♪ Bidibidibidibidibidibidi ♪

OH, WAIT, THAT'S MY CELL.

JUST A SEC.

SAVED BY THE BELL.

HELLO?

'LOOO?

FROM NOW ON, YOU ACT NICE TO YOUR MOM, OK?!

MORNING, MINA!

GOOD MORNING, MRS. GARSON!

THERE WAS MELON LEFT, SO I MADE SMOOTHIES!

HI, MOM?

YOU THERE?

HUH?

HELLO?

YO?

SPEAK UP...

GRNT!

I HATE YOU!!

MY REVENGE WILL BE TERRIBLE!

CAN I GIVE YOU A LITTLE SOMETHING FOR TOSSING HER IN THE POOL?

WE GOT CUT OFF.

RATS!

NO PROB, MR. HENRY. IT'S ON THE HOUSE.

THIS TIME.

LOU?

HELLO?

WHAT'S UP?

THE SIGNAL IS GONE...

THAT MEANS WE'RE HERE.

MORTSVILLE

I'M TELLING YOU, IT'S ALL GOING TO GO REALLY WELL.

WHAT? SO FAR THIS WHOLE TRIP IS A FAILURE! WE'RE TREATED LIKE DOGS, AND NO ONE TURNS UP TO MY BOOK SIGNINGS...

AND THIS PLACE'LL BE THE WORST OF ALL!

Book Fest

I GUESS IT'S FITTING THAT MORTSVILLE IS WHERE MY WRITING CAREER WILL OFFICIALLY DIE.

AND I BET MY MOTHER WILL BE THE FIRST ONE TO POINT OUT MY FAILURE.

THERE SHE IS!

AND-A-ONE, AND-A-TWO...

THERE'S MY GIRL!

WELCOME MORTSVILLE'S GREATEST AUTHOR

BOM

POM PA

BOM

19

THAT'S MY MOM.

HUH?

THAT BOOK YOU'RE READING. MY MOM WROTE IT.

WEIRD.

ARE YOU KIDDING ME?

NOPE.

THAT'S HER NAME? GRETEL BLONDILLA?

NO, THAT'S HER PSEUDONYM.

YOU MEAN...

WOW, THAT'S SO WILD...

HEY, MANNY. GUESS WHAT? LOU'S MOTHER WROTE SIDERA: GALACTIC ADVENTURES!

NO WAY!

WAY. HAVE YOU READ IT YET?

YOU BET! LOTS OF TIMES!

WE'RE BOTH HUGE FANS!

IT'S THE BEST BOOK SINCE SCROLL OF THE CYBER-POPES!

I HEARD SHE'S DOING A SIGNING AT THE CONVENTION OVER IN PINE RIDGE.

JUST DOWN THE SHORE.

YEAH, I KNOW. I WAS PLANNING TO MEET HER THERE...

GRETEL BLONDILLA'S DAUGHTER! WOW...

SO...YOU HAVE ANY GOOD STORIES ABOUT HER?

HA, LOTS, BUT...

GRUMBLE GRUMBLE

WHERE DID SHE GET ALL HER IDEAS FOR SIDERA?

WELL, WHEN I WAS LITTLE, SHE MADE UP LOTS OF BEDTIME STORIES FOR ME...

SHOW-OFF.

...AND OVER TIME, THE STORIES GOT BETTER AND BETTER...

...THEN ONE DAY, JUST TO SEE, SHE WROTE DOWN ONE OF HER STORIES AND SENT IT TO AN EDITOR, AND BOOM, HE LOVED IT AND ASKED FOR A WHOLE BOOK...

AND THAT'S IT!

IT'S FUNNY, BECAUSE THERE'S A LOT OF STUFF FROM OUR LIVES IN THERE, CHANGED A LITTLE BIT...

LIKE WHAT?

LIKE PRINCE FULGOR, IN THE BOOK, WAS BASED ON RICHARD, A REAL GUY IN HER LIFE...

HEY, GUYS, ARE YOU BUGGING HER ABOUT YOUR KIDDIE BOOK?

LOU DOESN'T WASTE HER TIME WITH THAT DUMB SCIENCE FICTION STUFF...

...THE SCIENCE FICTION LITERARY GENRE, SO DEAR TO OUR COMMUNITY, WHICH IS PROUD TO COUNT AMONG OUR OWN SUCH A YOUNG AND TALENTED AUTHOR...

...A COUNTRY GIRL, A MORTSVILLIAN IN HEART AND SOUL, WHO JOURNEYED TO THE BIG CITY TO RAISE HIGH THE FLAME OF OUR LOCAL CULTURE...

MY DAUGHTER.

YOU MUST BE PAUL. I'M RICHARD!

PLEASED TO MEET YOU. LOU TOLD ME A LOT ABOUT YOU.

FIFFER.

CLEMENT FIFFER.

WHATTA SHINDIG! THEY'VE GOT IT ALL!

SUPER KITSCHY!

MAJORETTES, EVEN!

WHAT, THE MAJORETTES?

COULD YOU WRITE, "FOR CLEMENT, MY DEAREST FRIEND"?

I DUNNO, THOSE MAJORETTES...

I'VE ALWAYS FOUND THEM KIND OF RIDICULOUS...

WHAT IS IT? AN ARMY? A DANCE? A SPORT?

AND THOSE ABSURD COSTUMES...

COMPANY...HALT!

AS THE FORMER CAPTAIN OF THE MORTSVILLE STARS, WILL YOU ACCEPT THE HONOR OF LEADING THE PARADE?

ONCE A STAR, ALWAYS A STAR!

COMPANY...MARCH!

SORRY, PAL...LOOKS LIKE YOU'VE PUT YOUR FOOT RIGHT IN IT.

YOU PUT YOUR FOOT IN IT.

HER MOM'S BOOK...

I REMEMBER NOW...

WHEN I USED TO LIVE ACROSS THE STREET...

IT'S THE BOOK SHE WAS TRYING TO WRITE...

Y'OKAY, I'M GOING TO HEAD INTO TOWN.

SEEYA LATER!

ARRRGH. I'M SUCH AN IDIOT!

...SO YOU SEE, IT'S NICE TO HAVE THESE LITTLE FANTASIES IN YOUR HEAD, BUT HERE'S THE TRUTH: HE JUST ISN'T THE RIGHT GUY FOR YOU!

SEE, HE WAS YOUR FIRST LOVE AND YOU MEET AGAIN BY CHANCE AND HE'S HOT AND THE SKY IS BLUE AND ALL THAT, SO OF COURSE YOU'RE ASKING YOURSELF IF THERE'S STILL ANYTHING BETWEEN YOU TWO...

YOU'RE LOOKING FOR CHEMISTRY...

BUT YOU HAVE TO ACCEPT THAT YOU AND HE AREN'T IN THE SAME WORLD ANYMORE...

IT'S TRUE, WHAT HE SAID ABOUT SCIENCE FICTION, THAT WAS LAME...

BUT YOU KNOW WHAT'S THE WORST IN ALL THIS?

...IT'S THAT I REALLY LIKE SCIENCE FICTION.

I DON'T KNOW WHY I SAID SOMETHING LIKE THAT!

SO YOU COULD LOOK LIKE THE BIG MATURE GUY, OF COURSE...

TO SHOW OFF.

YEP.

TRUST ME, DUDE. GIRLS LIKE GUYS WHO ACT NATURAL.

YEP.

NOW, TRISTAN, HE'S A GUY WITH HIS FEET ON THE GROUND, RIGHT? HE'S NOT THE TYPE WHO DAYDREAMS ABOUT THE COSMOS...

LOOK AT THE EVIDENCE. IT DIDN'T WORK OUT WITH YOU TWO THE FIRST TIME. THERE'S NO REASON YOU'LL FALL FOR EACH OTHER NOW.

YOU ARE IN-COM-PATIBLE.

HE'S NOT YOUR TYPE, THAT'S ALL.

SO WHAT IS MY TYPE, ACCORDING TO YOU?

I DUNNO. I GUESS DREAMERS, POETS, ROMANTICS...THAT KIND.

I'LL LEAVE THEM TO YOU...

?

I'M SUCH A JERK.

ONE DOES NOT SPEAK ILL OF THE MORTSVILLE STARS...

RIGHT. THEY'RE SACRED...

IT'S ALL OVER FOR YOU!

BUT I DIDN'T KNOW WHAT IT MEANT TO HER!

SHE'LL HATE ME NOW! BOOHOOHOO!

WELL, I HAVE TO GET BACK TO MY SALES BOOTH.

GET YER SIDERA T-SHIRTS, MOUSE PADS, DOILIES!

BOOHOO!

CHIN UP!

THERE, THERE...

YOU SHOULD JUST LEAVE.

YOU'VE DONE ENOUGH DAMAGE.

GO FAAAR AWAY...

HEY. PSST!

TA-DAA!

WHOA.

I TAKE BACK WHAT I SAID ABOUT THE COSTUME...

HE HE!

I FORGIVE YOU...

...AND I APOLOGIZE FOR...

WHOA.

♪ WOOOOOOHOO! ♫

CURSES. FOILED AGAIN.

BLAH BLAH PAUL BLAH BLAH BLAH BLAH BLAH PAUL!

OOO, LOOK, PAUL!

HA HA!

HEHE!

?

WHOO!

HEY, UH, GIRLS. WHAT WERE YOU SAYING ABOUT PAUL?

SHH!

JUST THAT HE'S THE CUTEST GUY IN TOWN!

MYSTERIOUS...

HUNKY...

ROMANTIC...

I HEAR HE PICKS HIS NOSE LIKE A PIG.

23

HOW LIKE A PIG?

LIKE THIS.

OIINK.

OH, MY WORD, YES, THAT'S DIS-GUST-ING!

AND IS THAT WHY YOU LOST INTEREST IN THIS CHRISTIAN?

TRISTAN.

OH, YES, TRISTAN.

UHM...NO, NOT REALLY, NOT FOR THAT...

...HE DID THAT BEFORE I WENT OUT WITH HIM...

...WHEN I WAS SPYING ON HIM WITH MY BINOCULARS FROM MY ROOF...

DEAR ME!

NO, THE THING THAT BROKE US UP WAS THAT LAME POSTCARD HE SENT LAST SUMMER.

AT LEAST HE WROTE...

ER...YEAH. BUT HE WROTE THIS STUPID THING, LIKE, "QUICK SMOOCH, STAY COOL..."

...ON A POSTCARD WITH AN UGLY MONKEY IN SWIM TRUNKS ON IT...

A MONKEY?

YES.

IMAGINE THAT.

AND THEN THAT WAS ALSO AT THE SAME TIME I MET PAUL...

PAUL? O-HO! ANOTHER LOVE AFFAIR?

OH, NO WAY.

AT LEAST, I DON'T THINK SO...

BUT PAUL...

WHEN HE SPEAKS, IT'S LIKE BEING TRANSPORTED...

...BUT WITH TRISTAN, NO LIFTOFF...

THE CONVERSATION ALWAYS STAYS ON THE GROUND...

AND YOU TOLD ME WHAT HE SAID ABOUT YOUR MOTHER'S BOOK. THAT'S REASON ENOUGH NOT TO LIKE THIS BOY...

RIGHT.

THAT SUMS IT UP, YEAH.

THERE'S JUST ONE LITTLE THING I DON'T UNDERSTAND...

...WHY HAVE YOU BEEN TALKING ABOUT HIM ALL MORNING LONG?

COME AND GET IT!

HEEENRY?

24

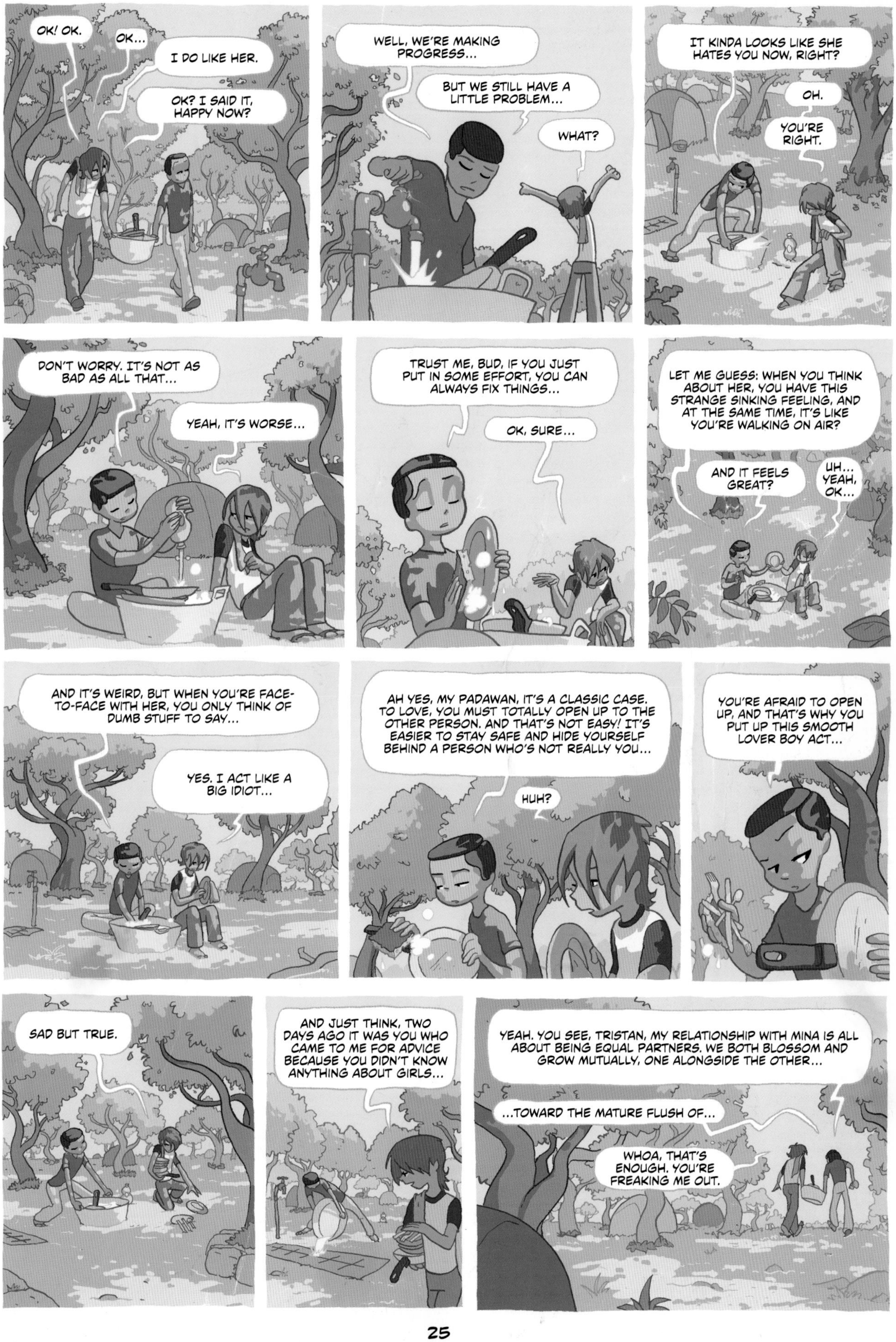

OK! OK.
OK...
I DO LIKE HER.
OK? I SAID IT, HAPPY NOW?
WELL, WE'RE MAKING PROGRESS...
BUT WE STILL HAVE A LITTLE PROBLEM...
WHAT?
IT KINDA LOOKS LIKE SHE HATES YOU NOW, RIGHT?
OH.
YOU'RE RIGHT.
DON'T WORRY. IT'S NOT AS BAD AS ALL THAT...
YEAH, IT'S WORSE...
TRUST ME, BUD, IF YOU JUST PUT IN SOME EFFORT, YOU CAN ALWAYS FIX THINGS...
OK, SURE...
LET ME GUESS: WHEN YOU THINK ABOUT HER, YOU HAVE THIS STRANGE SINKING FEELING, AND AT THE SAME TIME, IT'S LIKE YOU'RE WALKING ON AIR?
AND IT FEELS GREAT?
UH... YEAH, OK...
AND IT'S WEIRD, BUT WHEN YOU'RE FACE-TO-FACE WITH HER, YOU ONLY THINK OF DUMB STUFF TO SAY...
YES. I ACT LIKE A BIG IDIOT...
AH YES, MY PADAWAN, IT'S A CLASSIC CASE. TO LOVE, YOU MUST TOTALLY OPEN UP TO THE OTHER PERSON. AND THAT'S NOT EASY! IT'S EASIER TO STAY SAFE AND HIDE YOURSELF BEHIND A PERSON WHO'S NOT REALLY YOU...
HUH?
YOU'RE AFRAID TO OPEN UP, AND THAT'S WHY YOU PUT UP THIS SMOOTH LOVER BOY ACT...
SAD BUT TRUE.
AND JUST THINK, TWO DAYS AGO IT WAS YOU WHO CAME TO ME FOR ADVICE BECAUSE YOU DIDN'T KNOW ANYTHING ABOUT GIRLS...
YEAH. YOU SEE, TRISTAN, MY RELATIONSHIP WITH MINA IS ALL ABOUT BEING EQUAL PARTNERS. WE BOTH BLOSSOM AND GROW MUTUALLY, ONE ALONGSIDE THE OTHER...
...TOWARD THE MATURE FLUSH OF...
WHOA, THAT'S ENOUGH. YOU'RE FREAKING ME OUT.

I DON'T WANNA...

COME ON...

ON THE COUNT OF 3...

OK, BUT YOU'RE COMING WITH ME...

CRAZY Bikini SWIMWEAR

DING!

CAN I HELP YOU GUYS?

YES, HELLO, SIR, WE'D LIKE TO KNOW IF YOU HAVE FUR UNDERWEAR?

FOR MEN.

THAT'S NOT IN FASHION ANYMORE, YOU KNOW.

YES, BUT WE NEED IT FOR...

I'LL SEE WHAT I CAN DO FOR YOU!

CORINNE! DO WE STILL HAVE THOSE FUR PANTIES FROM LAST SUMMER IN THE BACK?

MANNY? PRESTON?

WHAT ARE YOU DOING HERE?

WE...WE...

WE CAN'T SAY... IT'S...

...IT'S TOP SECRET...

THAT'S IT!

AND WHAT ARE YOU...

I'M HELPING KAREN PICK OUT A--

I SWEAR, I CAN'T DO IT. IT'S TOO BEYONCÉ...

--BIKINI.

DON'T WORRY. YOU LOOK REALLY GREAT!

I'M LOVING IT...

TOPS!

JUST LIKE PRINCESS LEIA...

LOVE IT.

GENTLEMEN, YOU'RE IN LUCK. I HAVE JUST TWO LEFT!

WOULD YOU LIKE TO TRY THEM ON?

26

COME OOOON, YOU CAN TELL ME! WHAT ARE THE UNDERPANTS FOR?

UHHHH...

WE TOLD YOU. IT'S TOP SECRET.

FINE. SEE YOU.

LATER.

HEY, WHERE ARE YOU GOING ALL BY YOURSELF?

YOU'RE BUSY...

SEE YOU TONIGHT.

HEY!

HEY, LOVEBIRDS!

YOU BOUGHT THE FUR?

UH, YES, BUT THERE'S STILL SOME WORK TO DO ON IT...

OUR TOP SECRET THING...

WHAT ELSE DO YOU NEED? FEATHER BOAS?

HAR HAR, VERY FUNNY.

GOOD TIMING...

WE WANT TO TALK TO YOU ABOUT SOMETHING...

IN PRIVATE...

SO WE KNOW IT'S ONLY BEEN A FEW DAYS, BUT...

...BUT WE'VE DECIDED TO SYMBOLICALLY CELEBRATE OUR GOING OUT, WITH A LITTLE PARTY TOMORROW NIGHT...

RIGHT, MI AMOR?

OH, JUST A SIMPLE THING, WITH A BONFIRE, FRIENDS, MUSIC...

...A GIANT CAKE...

A GIANT CAKE?

PLEEEEASE?

OF COURSE, SWEETIE, WE'LL GET A GIANT CAKE...

I CAN'T RESIST THOSE EYES...

LAMB CHOP!

CUDDLE BUG!

CUDDLE LAMB!

SWEETIE PIE!

SNOOKUMS!

POOPSIE!

UM.

OH, ER, SORRY. SO...

WE'D LIKE TO KNOW IF YOU'D LIKE TO BE OUR MAID OF HONOR...?

YOU'VE GONE OFF THE DEEP END...

...WE ARE JOINED HERE AT THEIR REQUEST TO CELEBRATE THE INSUFFERABLE AND SUDDEN FUSION OF THE HEARTS OF GIANNI AND MINA...

...THEIR SILLY SHARED SMILES, THEIR CUTE LITTLE NICKNAMES... WE SHOULD BE SICK OF THEM, WE UNFORTUNATE SINGLE PEOPLE...

...BUT THEY ARE OUR FRIENDS, AND TONIGHT, I SUPPOSE THEY JUST WANT TO SHARE WITH US A LITTLE OF THE JOY THAT HAS SURROUNDED THEM THESE PAST FEW DAYS...THIS AMAZING THING THAT I HOPE WE'LL ALL FIND IN THE END: LOVE!

YOU MAY KISS THE... EACH OTHER!

MAY THEIR JOY SPLASH OVER US ALL!

CLAP!
CLAP!
CLAP!
CLAP!
CLAP!

OK. YOU CAN STOP KISSING NOW...

FETCH THE GIANT CAKE!

YAAHOOO!

YOUR SPEECH WAS SWEET...

VERY...UH... POETIC...

I ESPECIALLY LIKED:

"MAY THEIR JOY SPLASH OVER US ALL."

OH, REALLY? IT WAS A LITTLE SILLY, BUT IT SOUNDED GOOD, HUH?

RIGHT, SO...I WANTED TO TELL YOU...

...WHAT I SAID ABOUT YOUR MOTHER'S BOOK, THE OTHER DAY, I'M SORRY AND...

...AND ALSO...I'VE BEEN TRYING TO BE A LITTLE LESS...

A LITTLE LESS WHAT?

I DUNNO...BUT WHEN I SEE YOU I...I DUNNO HOW TO...UH...

COMMUNICATE?

YEAH...SOMETHING LIKE THAT. SO I PROMISED MYSELF THAT I'D TRY TO BE... NO, I'M GOING TO BE...UH...

MORE NATURAL?

THAT.

SO, OK, I...I'M BABBLING... I...

I SOUND LIKE AN IDIOT.

THEN BE QUIET.

SILENCE IS GOLDEN.

UH, TRUE...

RIGHT.

IT'S NOT SO BAD...

SHHH!

HAPPY COUPLE COMING THROUGH!

MAY THEIR JOY SPLASH OVER US ALL!

29

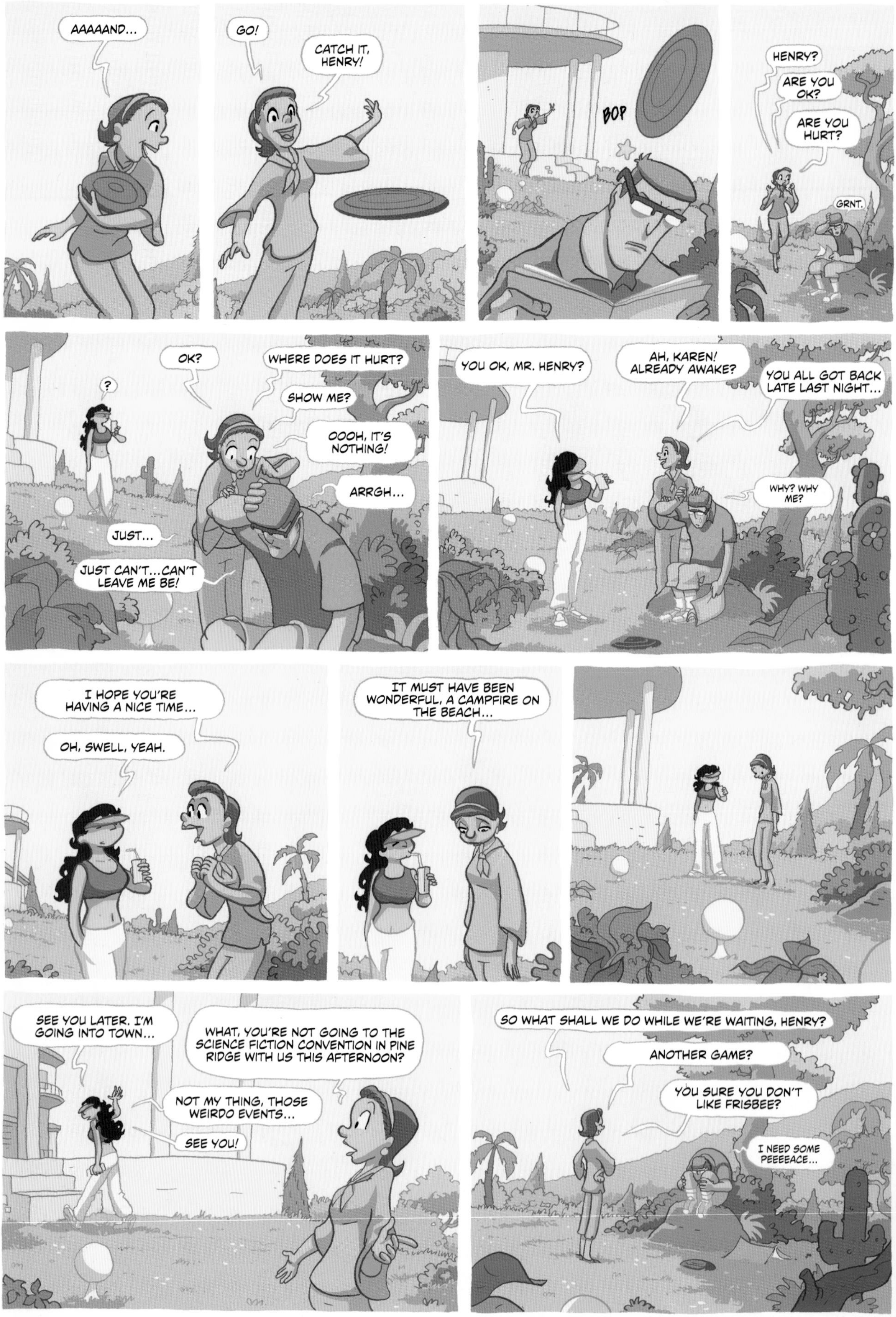

AAAAAND...
GO!
CATCH IT, HENRY!
BOP
HENRY?
ARE YOU OK?
ARE YOU HURT?
GRNT.
?
OK?
WHERE DOES IT HURT?
SHOW ME?
OOOH, IT'S NOTHING!
ARRGH...
JUST...
JUST CAN'T...CAN'T LEAVE ME BE!
YOU OK, MR. HENRY?
AH, KAREN! ALREADY AWAKE?
YOU ALL GOT BACK LATE LAST NIGHT...
WHY? WHY ME?
I HOPE YOU'RE HAVING A NICE TIME...
OH, SWELL, YEAH.
IT MUST HAVE BEEN WONDERFUL, A CAMPFIRE ON THE BEACH...
SEE YOU LATER. I'M GOING INTO TOWN...
WHAT, YOU'RE NOT GOING TO THE SCIENCE FICTION CONVENTION IN PINE RIDGE WITH US THIS AFTERNOON?
NOT MY THING, THOSE WEIRDO EVENTS...
SEE YOU!
SO WHAT SHALL WE DO WHILE WE'RE WAITING, HENRY?
ANOTHER GAME?
YOU SURE YOU DON'T LIKE FRISBEE?
I NEED SOME PEEEEACE...

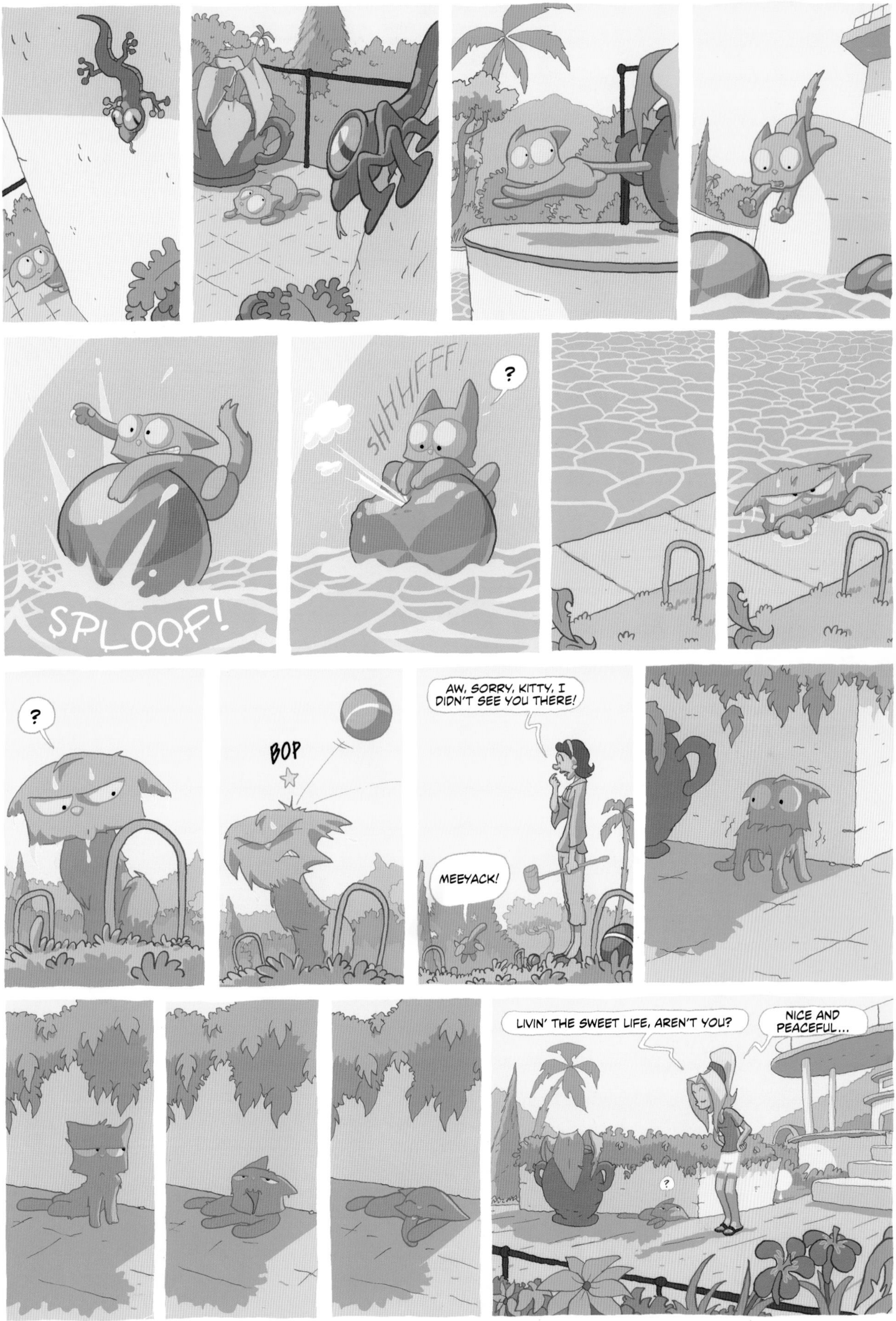
SPLOOF!
SHHHFFF!
?
?
BOP
AW, SORRY, KITTY, I DIDN'T SEE YOU THERE!
MEEYACK!
LIVIN' THE SWEET LIFE, AREN'T YOU?
NICE AND PEACEFUL...
?

GOT EVERYTHING?

THE FURS AND ALL?

READY, GUYS?

CHECK.

WHAT'S UP WITH THE GIRLS?

I CALLED MINA. WE'LL MEET THEM THERE. MARY EMILY'S MOTHER IS DROPPING THEM OFF AROUND 2.

LOOKS LIKE THINGS ARE GOING WELL WITH LOU, LATELY...

YEAH, IT'S WEIRD. BUT GOOD. BUT NOTHING'S HAPPENED YET.

HMM...I THINK IT WON'T BE LONG...

HEY, ARE YOU COMING WITH US TO THE CON?

DO YOU EVEN KNOW ME?

WHAT'S UP WITH THE GUYS? DID YOU REACH GIANNI?

YES, WE'LL MEET THEM THERE.

TRISTAN WILL DEFINITELY BE THERE.

HEE!

OK, OK, I'LL GO WITH YOU.

IT'LL BE STUPID, I'M SURE, BUT OK...

OH BOY, I'M GOING TO BE SO HAPPY TO SEE MY MOTHER AND RICHARD!

HI, SWEETUMS? YES, WE'RE HERE...

RIGHT, AT THE ENTRANCE.

HMM? WHAT'D YOU SAY, MY LOVELY?

WHAT? HOW CAN YOU BE AT THE ENTRANCE TOO?

UH...WE'RE TAKING OFF. WE'RE GOING TO LOOK FOR SOMEPLACE TO CHANGE...

SEE YOU SOON!

LISTEN, I'M NOT BEING STUPID! THERE'S A SIGN THAT SAYS ENTRANCE RIGHT HERE...

...MY BELOVED...

SO WHERE ARE THEY?

GIMME A SEC...

POOKIE? YOU'RE AT THE ENTRANCE WHERE YOU BUY TICKETS, RIGHT?

HUH? WHAT? YOU'RE AT THE OTHER ENTRANCE, INSIDE?

UH-HUH.

FINE, NO NEED TO GET ALL WORKED UP...

THIS IS LAME.

...SUGARBEAR.

OH, GOOD, I SEE YOU!

TRISTAN!

♪YOOHOO!♪

HOW WAS I SUPPOSED TO KNOW THERE WERE TWO ENTRANCES?

...BUNNYKINS.

UGH! YOU KNOW I DON'T LIKE IT, MUFFIN, WHEN YOU TREAT ME LIKE I'M STUPID...

SORRY, MY ANGEL.

FUNNY, WHO KNEW, BUT I LOVE SCIENCE FICTION!

YEAH?

COOL.

HEY!

SMACK!

WHAT'S UP?

SMACK!

OK, I NEED TO FIND THE PLACE WITH THE BOOK SIGNINGS...

RIGHT, AND FIND YOUR MOTHER...

OVER THERE, I THINK...

TRISTAN...

I THINK WE HAD A LITTLE... SWEET MOMENT THERE, DON'T YOU?

UH?

TRISTAN?

WHERE'D HE--

LOULOU!

MOM!

RICHARD!

HEY HEY!

HOW IS IT POSSIBLE? YOU'VE ALREADY GOTTEN BIGGER!

A LI'L.

OH! WAIT!

WE BROUGHT YOU A BIG SURPRISE IN OUR LUGGAGE...

READY? GET SET...

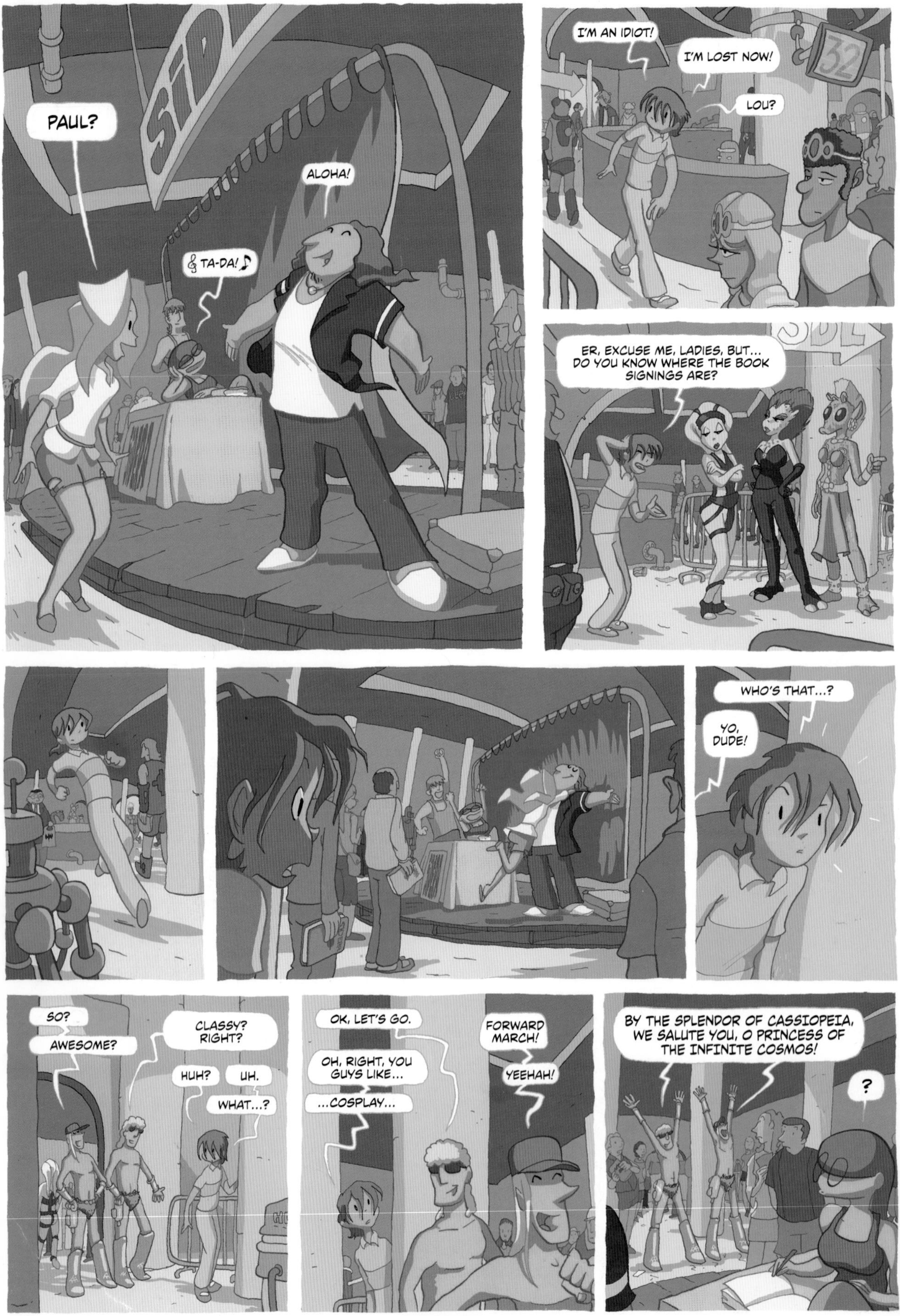
PAUL?
TA-DA!
ALOHA!
I'M AN IDIOT!
I'M LOST NOW!
LOU?
32
ER, EXCUSE ME, LADIES, BUT... DO YOU KNOW WHERE THE BOOK SIGNINGS ARE?
WHO'S THAT...?
YO, DUDE!
SO?
AWESOME?
CLASSY? RIGHT?
HUH?
UH.
WHAT...?
OK, LET'S GO.
OH, RIGHT, YOU GUYS LIKE...
...COSPLAY...
FORWARD MARCH!
YEEHAH!
BY THE SPLENDOR OF CASSIOPEIA, WE SALUTE YOU, O PRINCESS OF THE INFINITE COSMOS!
?

UM... ER...

HELLO, UM...

MOM, MEET MANNY AND PRESTON.

FRIENDS OF YOURS?

ER...YES.

DO THEY ALWAYS DRESS LIKE THAT?

NO...I DON'T GET IT...UH...

WHAT??! LOOK AT US!

DISINTEGRATOR GUNS...

THE SATURNIUM ARMBANDS...

THE ZNORG-SCALE BOOTS...

THE FUR UNDERPANTS!!

PRINCE FULGOR!

YOU'RE DRESSED AS PRINCE FULGORS!

WHEW!

OH...NOW THAT YOU SAY IT...

IT'S A SORT OF HOMAGE WE WANTED TO MAKE TO YOU...

...BECAUSE WE'RE SIDERA'S BIGGEST FANS...

I SEE. THANK YOU...

WE HONOR YOUR CHARACTERS!

I...I DON'T KNOW WHAT TO SAY...

IT TOOK A LOT OF WORK...

DO THOSE UNDERPANTS ITCH?

NOPE, THEY'RE REALLY COMFY.

MINE TICKLES A LITTLE.

SO, MANNY, AND PRESTON ARE FRIENDS OF TRISTAN...

HEHE!

TRISTAN?

WHO?

TRISTAN WHO LIVED ACROSS THE STREET?

RIGHT, THAT TRISTAN...

AND GET THIS: TURNS OUT HE'S ON VACATION HERE TOO...

TRISTAN WHO PLAYED VIDEO GAMES?

THAT'S RIGHT.

AND GUESS WHAT, I MET UP WITH HIM BY CHANCE...

TRISTAN YOUR FIRST LOVE?

WELL, YES, BUT...

A LOT HAS CHANGED SINCE THEN...

UM, CAN WE GET OUR BOOKS SIGNED?

?

"MAY THEIR JOY SPLASH OVER US..."

YEAH YEAH YEAH YEAH.

JOY, MY BUTT.

HEY, MARY EM...

TRISTAN?

MMMPH?

HUH?

WHAT?

I'M TELLING LOU!

NO, WAIT...

WHAT?

WHADDAYOUMEAN, "NO, WAIT"?

IF SHE FINDS OUT THAT HE...UM...

YOU'D BETTER BELIEVE SHE'S GOING TO FIND OUT!

JUST HOLD ON A MINUTE, PUMPKIN!

HE...HE GOT A BUMP ON THE HEAD. HE DOESN'T KNOW WHAT HE'S DOING...

I DON'T GET IT...

YOU'RE JUST MAKING UP EXCUSES.

DON'T TELL ME YOU'RE CONDONING YOUR PAL'S BEHAVIOR?

BUT ALL THE WAY HERE HE WAS TALKING ABOUT NOTHING BUT LOU, AND HE--

HEY, MINA! GIANNI!

THIS IS PAUL, MY GREAT FRIEND FROM MORTSVILLE!

P-PAUL? THE PAUL?

HEY!

BUT-BUT...WHAT?!

MY MOTHER INVITED HIM TO COME DOWN TO THE CON...

HI, MINA!

ENCHANTÉ!

ISN'T THAT MARY-WHOSIT'S MOTHER DOWN IN THE PARKING LOT?

YES, SHE CAME TO PICK US UP.

LET'S GO SAY HI.

SO...DO WE TELL HER OR NOT?

UH...I DUNNO, NOW...

YOOHOO!

CAN THEY SEE ME?

YOOHOO!

YOOHOO!

YOO--

OH, THEY SEE ME!

?

MARY...

IS THAT YOU?

WHAT...?

ARE YOU OK, HONEY?

LET IT GO.

ALLO ALLO! ♪

MRS. GARSON, MEET MY FRIEND PAUL...

AN HONOR...

UH...UM...

HELLO, EVERYONE!

SO? HOW WAS YOUR DAY?

MEH, I SPENT THE WHOLE TIME STUCK INDOORS...

THEN YOU HAVE TO COME TO THE COTTAGE. THIS AREA IS SOOO PRETTY, YOU KNOW...

ALL THE STONE TERRACES...

UNFORTUNATELY, WE LEAVE TOMORROW MORNING...

MARY EMILY, PAUL...

I TOLD YOU ABOUT HIM, I THINK.

UH-HUH.

YOU MUST BE HER FAT FRIEND FROM THE STICKS?

AND I GUESS YOU'RE HER SPOILED FRIEND WHO PLAYS AT BEING A REBEL?

JUST LET IT PASS...

HOW'D YOU GET TO BE FRIENDS WITH THAT...

IN SIX STEPS: DENIAL, ANGER, BARGAINING, DEPRESSION, ACCEPTANCE, AND FINALLY FRIENDSHIP.

YOU HAVEN'T SEEN TRISTAN, BY ANY CHANCE?

HE JUST LEFT A MINUTE AGO!

EVERYTHING GOING OK WITH THE GIRLS?

OH, YOU KNOW, I'VE STAYED OUT OF THEIR WAY...

...ALWAYS RUNNING HERE AND THERE...

...KIDS, YOU KNOW...

SAY, I'VE JUST HAD A THOUGHT: WHY DON'T YOU TWO STAY OVER A FEW DAYS AT OUR PLACE?

WELL, THAT'S...

YOU'LL LOVE OUR VILLA!

WE WOULDN'T WANT TO TROUBLE YOU...

PLEEEEEEASE?

HI, POPS!

YES, IT'S ME.

REALLY GOOD...

WHAT'S UP?

I'VE BEEN INVITED TO STAY A FEW DAYS AT LOU'S FRIEND'S...

YES.

NO, DON'T WORRY...

THANKS, POPS!

LATER...

CIAO!

HERE YOU GO. THANKS FOR THE PHONE!

AND FOR THE HOSPITALITY!

AND FOR THE ROBE!

THANK MY WIFE...

SPLOOF!

WELL, HELLO!

SO...TELL ME...

HOW OLD IS YOUR FRIEND PAUL?

ER...FIFTEEN...

DUNNO...

FIFTEEN...?

WELL, YOU'RE NOT ALL THAT BAD!

HUH? UH, THANKS.

DOWN, GIRL...

YOU PLANNING TO KISS HIM TOO?

HAVE YOU LOST IT?

BACK OFF...

ANYWAY, IT'S TRISTAN WHO KISSED ME.

YEAH. BUT YOU DIDN'T LOOK LIKE YOU MINDED IT TOO MUCH...

ENTHUSIASTICALLY...

RIGHT, MINA?

HECK YES. NO QUALMS. REAL DIRECT.

COMPARED TO LOU, ANYWAY...

HEY, THAT'S HOW THE BOY HUNT WORKS! EVERY GIRL FOR HERSELF. THAT GIVES ME ONE POINT...

MINA HAS ONE POINT TOO.

NONE OF YOUR BUSINESS.

LOU, ZERO.

AND KAREN?

JUST GO ON AS IF I'M NOT HERE...

HEY!

?

?

?

?

SPLASH!

LOU?

BUT...WHAT...?

SMOOCH!

!

!

!

OH, LOOK: YOUR DAUGHTER IS KISSING HER BEST FRIEND ON THE MOUTH...

OH.

AS I PLANNED.

BUT I THOUGHT THEY WERE JUST FRIENDS, NOTHING MORE...

PFFT. SO YOU THOUGHT!

HAAAAAROOOMPH!

MORNING, EVERYBODY!

LOOK AT THEM...IT'S ALL A BIG MESS...

YOU SAID IT!

A DISASTER...

...PATHETIC...

THEY HAVE TO GET TOGETHER...

...TRISTAN AND LOU...

...IT'S DESTINY...

BUT, THEN, SHE WENT OFF WITH THAT HULA SKIRT GUY THERE...

HE'S REALLY JUST A FRIEND...

...NOTHING MORE...

OK. I SEE HOW IT IS: SHE'S YOUR FRIEND, SO YOU GIVE HER EVERY EXCUSE IN THE BOOK.

BUT IF SHE'S GOING OUT WITH PAUL, I TOLD YOU IT'S BECAUSE YOUR BUDDY TRISTAN IS ALL OVER MARY EMILY...

HEY, WAIT A MINUTE HERE. YOU'RE GOING ON ABOUT YOUR TWO HEROES, LIKE THEY'RE THE ONLY ONES IN THIS RIDICULOUS SITUATION!

AND THE TWO REAL VICTIMS ARE REALLY PAUL AND MARY EMILY...

ABSOLUTELY. PLAYING LIKE THAT WITH THEIR FEELINGS. I FIND IT COMPLETELY DISGUSTING.

INDEED.

I...I NEVER LOOKED AT IT LIKE THAT...

CLASSIC. WHO CARES ABOUT ANYONE ELSE, THEY'RE JUST SUPPORTING CHARACTERS...

YOU'RE STILL WEARING YOUR COSTUMES?

THEY'RE COMFY.

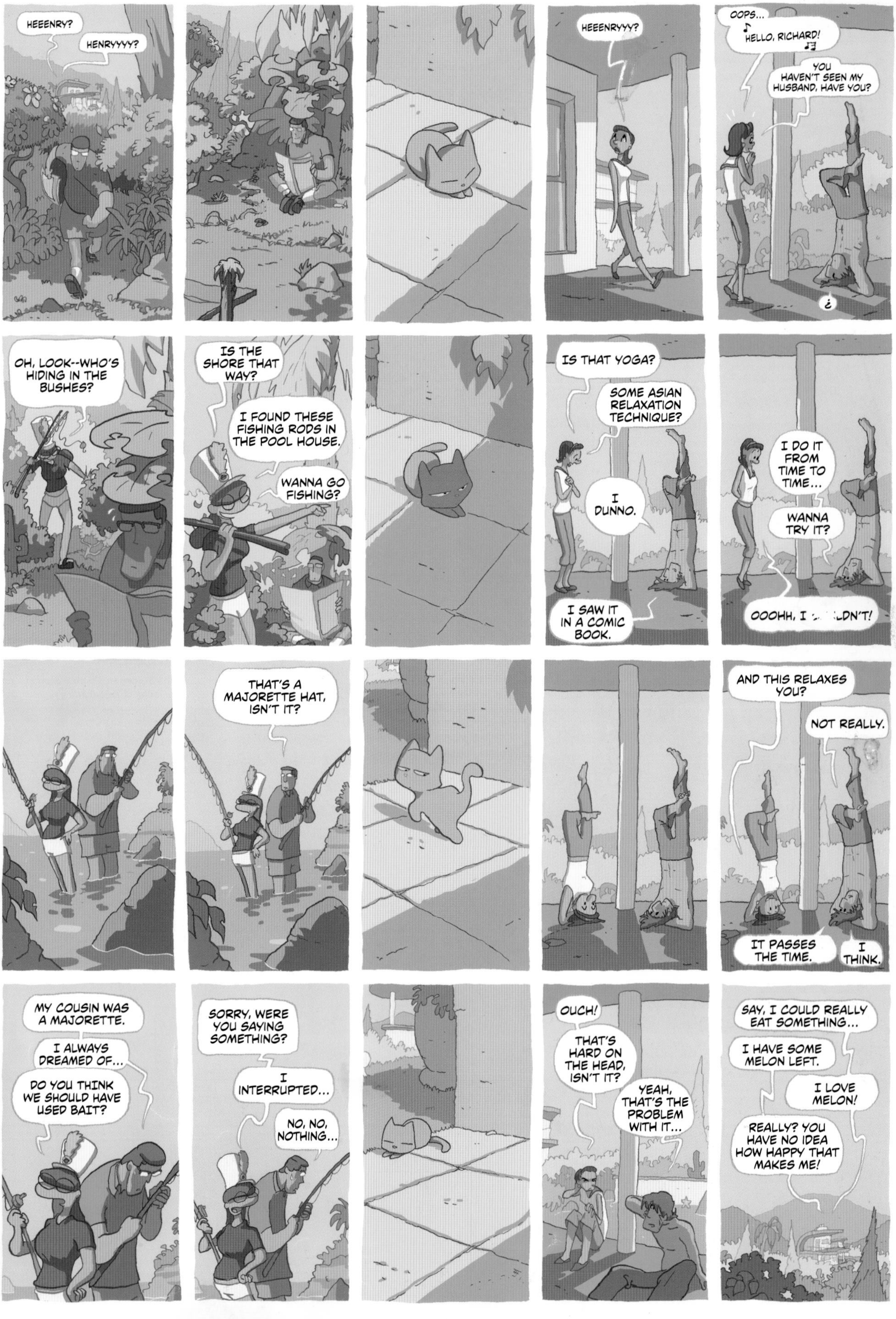
HEEENRY?
HENRYYYY?
HEEENRYYY?
OOPS...
HELLO, RICHARD!
YOU HAVEN'T SEEN MY HUSBAND, HAVE YOU?
¿
OH, LOOK--WHO'S HIDING IN THE BUSHES?
IS THE SHORE THAT WAY?
I FOUND THESE FISHING RODS IN THE POOL HOUSE.
WANNA GO FISHING?
IS THAT YOGA?
SOME ASIAN RELAXATION TECHNIQUE?
I DUNNO.
I SAW IT IN A COMIC BOOK.
I DO IT FROM TIME TO TIME...
WANNA TRY IT?
OOOHH, I
LDN'T!
THAT'S A MAJORETTE HAT, ISN'T IT?
AND THIS RELAXES YOU?
NOT REALLY.
IT PASSES THE TIME.
I THINK.
MY COUSIN WAS A MAJORETTE.
I ALWAYS DREAMED OF...
DO YOU THINK WE SHOULD HAVE USED BAIT?
SORRY, WERE YOU SAYING SOMETHING?
I INTERRUPTED...
NO, NO, NOTHING...
OUCH!
THAT'S HARD ON THE HEAD, ISN'T IT?
YEAH, THAT'S THE PROBLEM WITH IT...
SAY, I COULD REALLY EAT SOMETHING...
I HAVE SOME MELON LEFT.
I LOVE MELON!
REALLY? YOU HAVE NO IDEA HOW HAPPY THAT MAKES ME!

...AND THEN THERE'S MY MOM...I DON'T KNOW WHAT HER PROBLEM IS...

...I DON'T UNDERSTAND HER AT ALL...

LIKE, Y'KNOW?

MMM...

SO.

SURE, IN MY FAMILY, WE'RE, LIKE, NOT EXACTLY COMMUNICATION CHAMPS...

GRNT...

GRNT...

IT'S FUNNY...BEFORE YOU MADE THE FIRST MOVE, I NEVER THOUGHT OF YOU AS A POTENTIAL GIRLFRIEND... IN MY MIND, YOU WERE STILL THE LITTLE GIRL ASLEEP IN THE MIDDLE OF A BIG FIELD...

THAT SEEMS SO LONG AGO...

BUT IT'S ONLY BEEN A YEAR...

ARE YOU LISTENING TO ME AT ALL?

HUH?

UM?

YEAH!

OK. IN THAT CASE, I'LL TELL YOU A SECRET.

I DON'T MIND PLAYING THE PART OF THE MEAN GIRL. IT'S FUN...

BUT I NEVER WANT TO PLAY THE PART OF AN IDIOT. NOR A VICTIM...

...AND YOU'RE NOT ANY FUN. YOU BORE ME.

I'M GONE.

CIAO, LOVER.

HUH?

HEY, PAUL?

YES?

YOU KNOW, WHEN I KISSED YOU, IT WAS, UM...

WHAT?

MAYBE A LITTLE BIT HASTY...

MAYBE NOT FOR THE RIGHT REASONS...

♪ Bidibidibidibidibidibi !♫

?

HELLO?

NO, I...

WHAT?

MINA NEEDS ME!

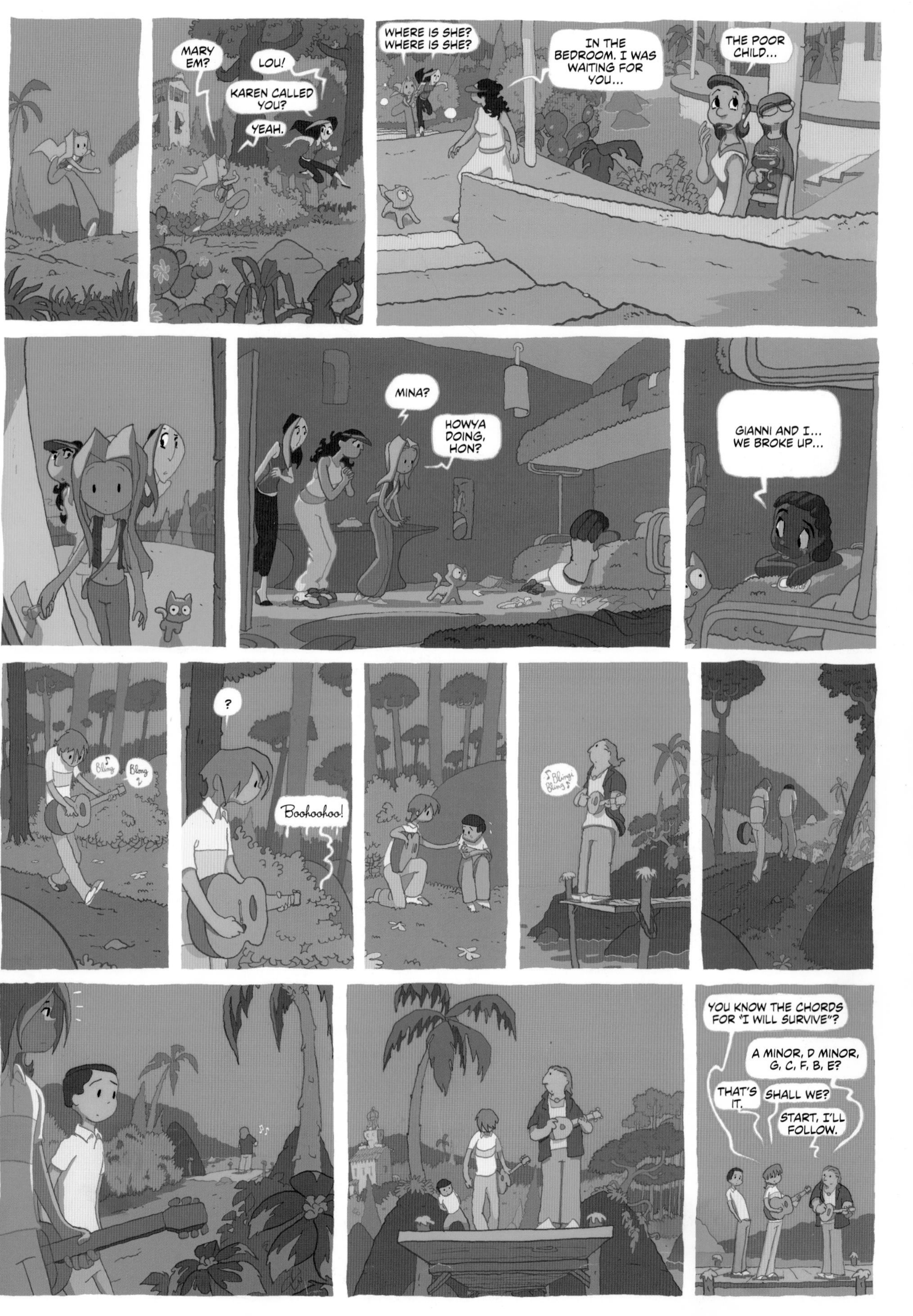
MARY EM?
LOU!
KAREN CALLED YOU?
YEAH.
WHERE IS SHE? WHERE IS SHE?
IN THE BEDROOM. I WAS WAITING FOR YOU...
THE POOR CHILD...
MINA?
HOWYA DOING, HON?
GIANNI AND I... WE BROKE UP...
Bling
Blong
?
Boohoohoo!
Bling Bling
YOU KNOW THE CHORDS FOR "I WILL SURVIVE"?
A MINOR, D MINOR, G, C, F, B, E?
THAT'S IT.
SHALL WE?
START, I'LL FOLLOW.

HAPPY BIRTHDAY
HAPPY, HAPPY
BIRTHDAY
HAPPY, HAPPY, HAPPY
BIRTHDAY

?

MOM?

YUP.

WHA' IS IT?

IT'S TODAY.

COOL, HUH?

?

HUH?

YOU'RE FOURTEEN.

?

Happy birthday!

WE'VE PUT TOGETHER A LITTLE PARTY FOR YOU!

ALL PLANNED WITH YOUR MOTHER.

AND YOU CAN EVEN INVITE THOSE BOYS WITH THE VESPAS...

YEAH!

?

SHE TALKED ME INTO IT.

?

THANKS, I...

IT WAS GOING TO BE A SURPRISE, BUT I WANTED TO WISH YOU HAPPY BIRTHDAY FIRST THING.

HA.

BREAKFAST!

OK.

I'M GOING BACK TO BED.

TEA?

ORANGE JUICE?

COFFEE?

CROISSANT?

COFFEE!

44

SO...

HAPPY BIRTHDAY!

IT WAS JUST A KISS, RIGHT?

NOTHING MORE?

OPEN IT WHEN YOU GET HOME.

PAUL, I'M SORRY. I RUINED EVERYTHING. NONO NONO!

STOP THAT!

IT'S ALL FORGOTTEN!

REALLY?

NO, NOT REALLY. OUR FRIENDSHIP WILL PROBABLY ALWAYS BE ONE OF THE BEST MEMORIES OF MY LIFE.

NEED A HAND?

OH, GOOD, A VOLUNTEER!

YOU THINK...?

GO ON.

IT'LL BE GREAT.

Welcome, welcome!

UH...

Hello, ma'am....

UH...

We brought flowers...

TRISTAN!

HEY!

FINALLY, I GET TO SEE YOU!

WOW! YOU GOT BIG!

...THINK WE CAN STILL STAY FRIENDS?

THAT'D BE OK WITH ME...

I DON'T THINK SHE REMEMBERS US.

YOUR ATTENTION, PLEASE.

SINCE THIS IS A PARTY AND ALL, I HAVE SOMEONE I'D LIKE YOU TO MEET.

SOMEONE I LIKE A LOT.

IF I HAVEN'T BEEN HANGING AROUND MUCH LATELY, IT'S BECAUSE I'VE BEEN GOING INTO TOWN IN THE AFTERNOON...

JUST LIKE THAT, ALL QUICKLY AND QUIETLY.

AND THEN, WELL...WE HAD SOME GOOD CHATS AND ALL THAT...

YOU CAN COME OUT! DON'T BE SCARED!

HEY, ALL...

HE'S SHY.

I THINK SHE WON THE BOY HUNT.

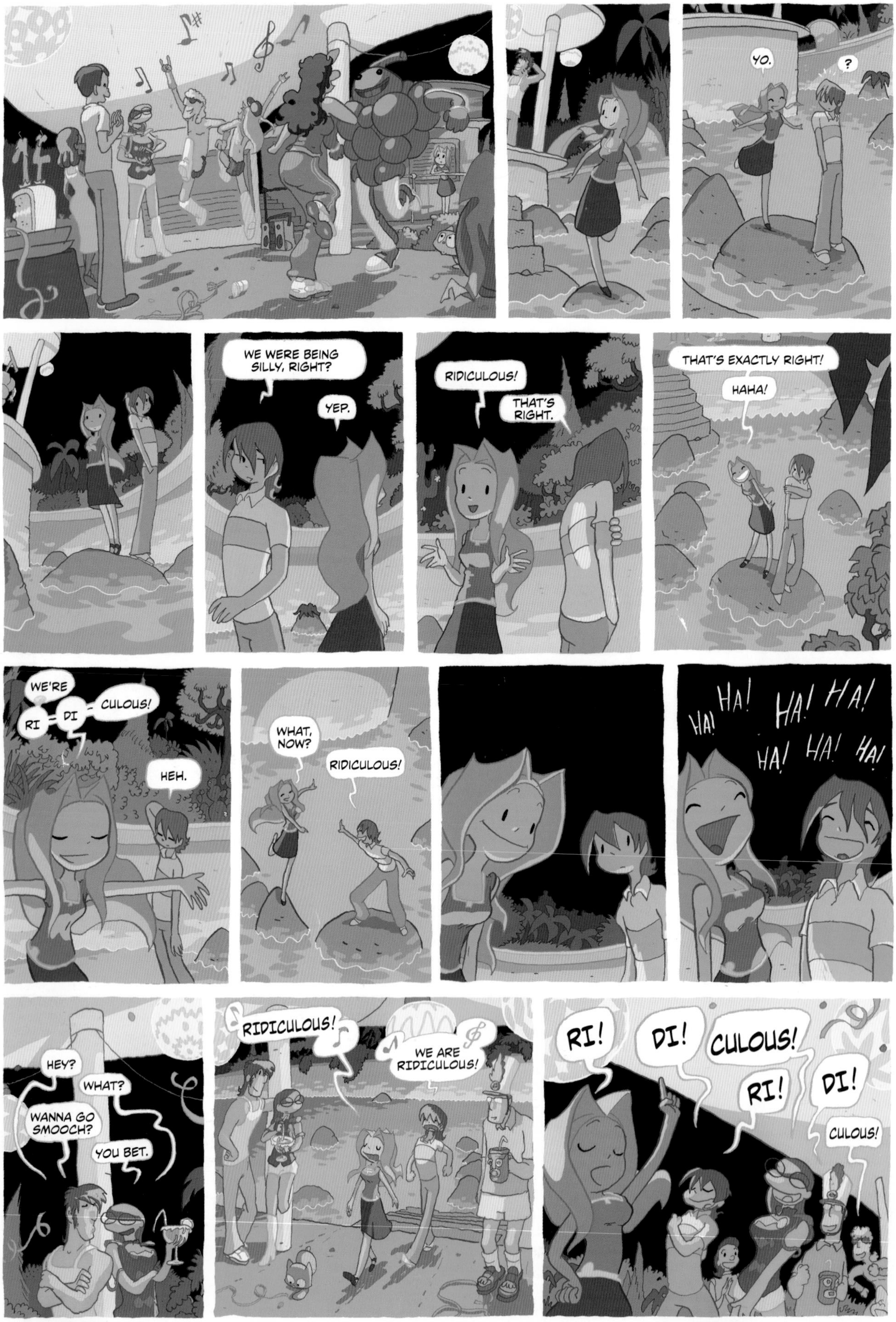
YO.
?
WE WERE BEING SILLY, RIGHT?
YEP.
RIDICULOUS!
THAT'S RIGHT.
THAT'S EXACTLY RIGHT!
HAHA!
WE'RE
RI
DI
CULOUS!
HEH.
WHAT, NOW?
RIDICULOUS!
HA! HA! HA! HA!
HA! HA! HA!
HEY?
WHAT?
WANNA GO SMOOCH?
YOU BET.
RIDICULOUS!
WE ARE RIDICULOUS!
RI!
DI!
CULOUS!
RI!
DI!
CULOUS!

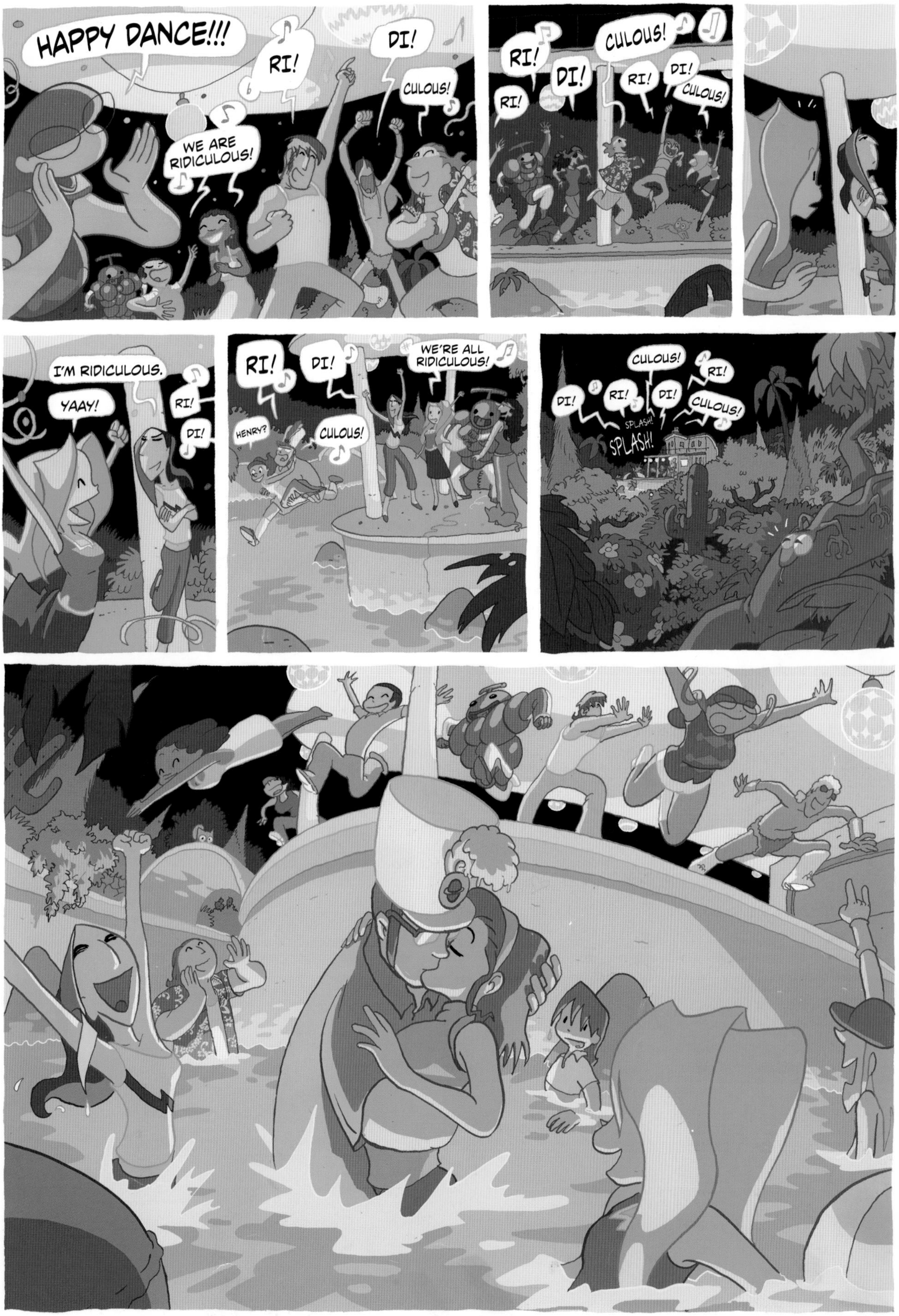
HAPPY DANCE!!!
RI!
DI!
CULOUS!
WE ARE RIDICULOUS!
RI!
RI!
DI!
CULOUS!
RI!
DI!
CULOUS!
I'M RIDICULOUS.
YAAY!
RI!
DI!
RI!
DI!
WE'RE ALL RIDICULOUS!
HENRY?
CULOUS!
DI!
RI!
CULOUS!
DI!
RI!
CULOUS!
SPLASH!
SPLASH!

SO DID YOU KISS TRISTAN OR NOT?

NO.

I DON'T THINK WE WERE READY YET...

...OR SOMETHING LIKE THAT...

HE'S INVITED ME TO GO ON A SKI TRIP WITH HIM THIS WINTER... THAT'LL BE NICE...

WHEN YOU BROUGHT PAUL TO THE CONVENTION...I DON'T KNOW IF THAT WAS A DISASTER OR A GOOD THING...

ANYWAY, DON'T SPRING ANYTHING LIKE THAT ON ME AGAIN.

UNDERSTOOD!

BUT DID YOU HAVE A GOOD VACATION ANYWAY?

I DIDN'T MESS IT ALL UP...?

NO, IT WAS SUPER.

SUPER!

WHEW.

THAT'S A RELIEF.

THIS COLD IS LAME.

I DON'T LIKE THE FALL.

I'M GOING IN.

I'M COMING.

SUPER.

The original back cover of the French edition

ARGH!
14 YEARS OLD!
I am oooold! (like Old Mother Hubbard!)

My BIRTHDAY CARD!
(which is OVER!)

signed by everybody during vacation!

...Some li'l pics of some new people in my li'l world!

First off:

MR. HENRY

After my birthday party, he had a sort of revelation or something...
He was in a good mood for the rest of the stay.
Well...good for him!

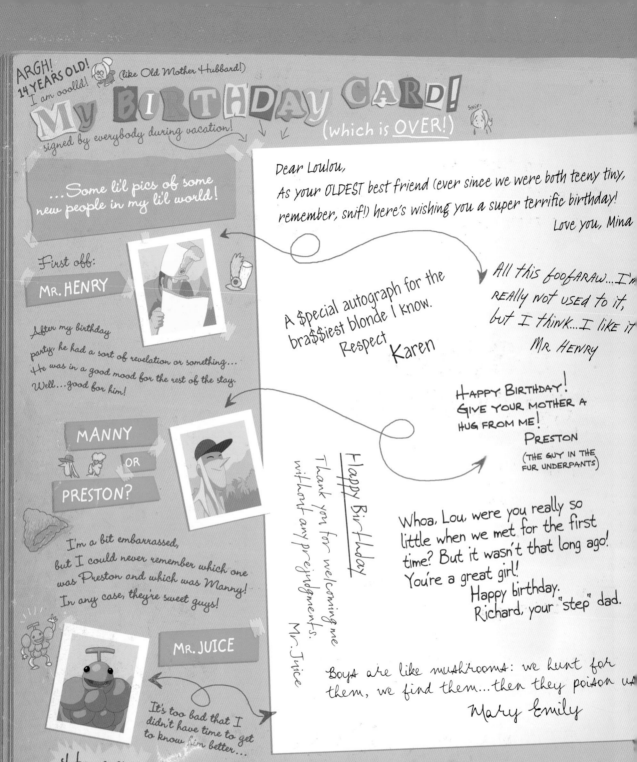

MANNY OR PRESTON?

I'm a bit embarrassed, but I could never remember which one was Preston and which was Manny! In any case, they're sweet guys!

MR. JUICE

It's too bad that I didn't have time to get to know him better...

However:

He helped me out at the end of the trip by getting THE ANIMAL back in his carrier.
SEE INTELLIGENCE REPORT / 545-P

Dear Loulou,
As your OLDEST best friend (ever since we were both teeny tiny, remember, snif!) here's wishing you a super terrific birthday!
Love you, Mina

A $pecial autograph for the bra$$iest blonde I know.
Respect Karen

All this foofaraw...I'm really not used to it, but I think...I like it
MR. HENRY

HAPPY BIRTHDAY!
GIVE YOUR MOTHER A HUG FROM ME!
PRESTON
(THE GUY IN THE FUR UNDERPANTS)

Happy Birthday
Thank you for welcoming me without any prejudgments.
Mr. Juice

Whoa, Lou, were you really so little when we met for the first time? But it wasn't that long ago! You're a great girl!
Happy birthday.
Richard, your "step" dad.

Boys are like mushrooms: we hunt for them, we find them...then they poison us
Mary Emily

BOOO!
terrified

Kitty kitty kitty!

GOTCHA!
ZIIP!
WHACK!

THANKS!
MISTER JUICE: ALWAYS READY TO HELP!
MEOW!

3 1170 00896 3377